'He can spring revelations on you in a single phrase. A master of timing, he can turn a character inside out in one fluid move . . . It's as if the literary equivalent of the Fibonacci series governs the patterns Salter creates' *Sunday Herald*

'There is a deadly hum of eroticism beneath his narrative and in the voluptuous restraint of his style. These stories span decades, whole lives. What else can I say? I highly recommend it' Charlotte Hobson, *Daily Telegraph*

'Breathtaking . . . Salter's stories are masterpieces of poise and clarity, so much so that their dazzling surface stillness often blinds you to the surprisingly bold risks . . . hugely enjoyable and endlessly stimulating' *Metro*

'A gut-punching work of genius' *Dazed & Confused*

'Terrific fiction, written by an important writer . . . All of these stories share Salter's exquisite prose, his talent for flitting gracefully between points of view, his uncanny ability to sum up a character in a single detail . . . These stories should be read and savored' *Washington Post*

'Life is a volatile mess, and no one portrays that mess better than James Salter . . . All of the stories in *Last Night* are superb' *New York Times Book Review*

'A glowing gem in Salter's remarkable body of work. *Last Night* should be X-rated, not for its eroticism, although there is that, but to forewarn the uninitiated of its scalding truths about the deceptions and devastations of love . . . Beyond the purity of language and the skill, each story has at its heart an underlying sensibility that treasures each moment of beauty, each burning day . . . Astonishing, haunting, heartbreaking'   *Los Angeles Times Book Review*

'Exquisite, pitch-perfect, timeless . . . You can practically smell the cigarette smoke and hear the booze-scratched timbre of Salter's characters' voices . . . In this era of chatter and distraction, Salter's carefully honed stories offer a welcome precision'   *San Francisco Chronicle*

'The maestro constantly stirs you as you read . . . The sentences alone create a certain breathlessness. Paradise, in Salter's fiction, has always already been lost. Yet the memory of a greener time persists, if only in his prose. While reading it, how happy one is'   *Chicago Tribune*

LAST NIGHT

JAMES SALTER is the author of numerous books, including the novels *Solo Faces*, *Light Years*, *A Sport and a Pastime*, *The Arm of Flesh* (revised as *Cassada*), and *The Hunters*; the memoirs *Gods of Tin* and *Burning the Days*; the collections *Dusk and Other Stories*, which won the 1989 PEN/Faulkner Award, and *Last Night*, which won the Rea Award for the Short Story and the PEN/Malamud Award; and *Life Is Meals: A Food Lover's Book of Days*, written with Kay Salter. He lives in New York and Colorado.

JAMES SALTER

LAST NIGHT

PICADOR

First published 2005 as a Borzoi Book by Alfred A. Knopf,
a division of Random House, Inc., New York,
and simultaneously in Canada by Random House of Canada Limited

First published in the UK 2006 by Picador

This edition published 2014 by Picador
an imprint of Pan Macmillan, a division of Macmillan Publishers Limited
Pan Macmillan, 20 New Wharf Road, London N1 9RR
Basingstoke and Oxford
Associated companies throughout the world
www.panmacmillan.com

ISBN 978-1-4472-5072-2

The acknowledgements on page viii constitute an extension of this copyright page.

1 3 5 7 9 8 6 4 2

A CIP catalogue record for this book is available from the British Library.

Printed and bound by CPI Group (UK) Ltd, Croydon, CR0 4YY

GEORGE PLIMPTON

hadada

Some of the stories in this collection previously appeared in
the following:
'My Lord You' and 'Comet' in *Esquire*,
'Arlington' in *Hartford Courant Literary Supplement*,
'Last Night' in the *New Yorker*, 'Bangkok' in the *Paris Review*,
'Give' and 'Such Fun' in *Tin House*, and 'Eyes of the Stars' in *Zoetrope*.
Six of the stories in this collection previously appeared in
Bangkok by Editions des Deux Terres, Paris, in 2003.

Contents

LAST NIGHT

Comet

<hr/>

PHILIP MARRIED ADELE on a day in June. It was cloudy and the wind was blowing. Later the sun came out. It had been a while since Adele had married and she wore white: white pumps with low heels, a long white skirt that clung to her hips, a filmy blouse with a white bra underneath, and around her neck a string of freshwater pearls. They were married in her house, the one she'd gotten in the divorce. All her friends were there. She believed strongly in friendship. The room was crowded.

— I, Adele, she said in a clear voice, give myself to you, Phil, completely as your wife . . . Behind her as best man, somewhat oblivious, her young son was standing, and pinned to her panties as something borrowed was a small silver disc, actually a St. Christopher's medal her father had worn in the war; she had several times rolled down the waistband of her skirt to show it to people. Near the door, under the impression that she was part of a garden tour, was an old woman who held a little dog by the handle of a cane hooked through his collar.

LAST NIGHT

At the reception Adele smiled with happiness, drank too
much, laughed, and scratched her bare arms with long show-
girl nails. Her new husband admired her. He could have
licked her palms like a calf does salt. She was still young
enough to be good-looking, the final blaze of it, though she
was too old for children, at least if she had anything to say
about it. Summer was coming. Out of the afternoon haze she
would appear, in her black bathing suit, limbs all tan, the
brilliant sun behind her. She was the strong figure walking up
the smooth sand from the sea, her legs, her wet swimmer's
hair, the grace of her, all careless and unhurried.

They settled into life together, hers mostly. It was her furniture and her books, though they were largely unread. She
liked to tell stories about DeLereo, her first husband—Frank,
his name was—the heir to a garbage-hauling empire. She
called him Delerium, but the stories were not unaffectionate.
Loyalty—it came from her childhood as well as the years of
marriage, eight exhausting years, as she said—was her code.
The terms of marriage had been simple, she admitted. Her
job was to be dressed, have dinner ready, and be fucked once
a day. One time in Florida with another couple they chartered
a boat to go bonefishing off Bimini.

— We'll have a good dinner, DeLereo had said happily, get
on board and turn in. When we get up we'll have passed the
Gulf Stream.

It began that way but ended differently. The sea was very
rough. They never did cross the Gulf Stream—the captain was
from Long Island and got lost. DeLereo paid him fifty dollars
to turn over the wheel and go below.

— Do you know anything about boats? the captain asked.

4

— More than you do, DeLereo told him.

He was under an ultimatum from Adele, who was lying, deathly pale, in their cabin. — Get us into port somewhere or get ready to sleep by yourself, she'd said.

Philip Ardet had heard the story and many others often. He was mannerly and elegant, his head held back a bit as he talked, as though you were a menu. He and Adele had met on the golf course when she was learning to play. It was a wet day and the course was nearly empty. Adele and a friend were teeing off when a balding figure carrying a cloth bag with a few clubs in it asked if he could join them. Adele hit a pass-able drive. Her friend bounced his across the road and teed up another, which he topped. Phil, rather shyly, took out an old three wood and hit one two hundred yards straight down the fairway.

That was his persona, capable and calm. He'd gone to Princeton and been in the navy. He looked like someone who'd been in the navy, Adele said—his legs were strong. The first time she went out with him, he remarked it was a funny thing, some people liked him, some didn't.

— The ones that do, I tend to lose interest in.

She wasn't sure just what that meant but she liked his appearance, which was a bit worn, especially around the eyes. It made her feel he was a real man, though perhaps not the man he had been. Also he was smart, as she explained it, more or less the way professors were.

To be liked by her was worthwhile but to be liked by him seemed somehow of even greater value. There was something about him that discounted the world. He appeared in a way to care nothing for himself, to be above that.

He didn't make much money, as it turned out. He wrote for a business weekly. She earned nearly that much selling houses. She had begun to put on a little weight. This was a few years after they were married. She was still beautiful—her face was—but she had adopted a more comfortable outline. She would get into bed with a drink, the way she had done when she was twenty-five. Phil, a sport jacket over his pajamas, sat reading. Sometimes he walked that way on their lawn in the morning. She sipped her drink and watched him.

— You know something?

— What?

— I've had good sex since I was fifteen, she said.

He looked up.

— I didn't start quite that young, he confessed.

— Maybe you should have.

— Good advice. Little late though.

— Do you remember when we first got started?

— I remember.

— We could hardly stop, she said. You remember?

— It averages out.

— Oh, great, she said.

After he'd gone to sleep she watched a movie. The stars grew old, too, and had problems with love. It was different, though—they had already reaped huge rewards. She watched, thinking. She thought of what she had been, what she had had. She could have been a star.

What did Phil know—he was sleeping.

AUTUMN CAME. One evening they were at the Morrisseys'— Morrissey was a tall lawyer, the executor of many estates and trustee of others. Reading wills had been his true education, a look into the human heart, he said.

At the dinner table was a man from Chicago who'd made a fortune in computers, a nitwit it soon became apparent, who during the meal gave a toast,

— To the end of privacy and the life of dignity, he said.

He was with a dampened woman who had recently found out that her husband had been having an affair with a black woman in Cleveland, an affair that had somehow been going on for seven years. There may even have been a child.

— You can see why coming here is like a breath of fresh air for me, she said.

The women were sympathetic. They knew what she had to do—she had to rethink completely the past seven years.

— That's right, her companion agreed.

— What is there to be rethought? Phil wanted to know.

He was answered with impatience. The deception, they said, the deception—she had been deceived all that time. Adele meanwhile was pouring more wine for herself. Her napkin covered the place where she had already spilled a glass of it.

— But that time was spent in happiness, wasn't it? Phil asked guilelessly. That's been lived. It can't be changed. It can't be just turned into unhappiness.

— That woman stole my husband. She stole everything he had vowed.

— Forgive me, Phil said softly. That happens every day.

There was an outcry as if from a chorus, heads thrust forward like the hissing, sacred geese. Only Adele sat silent.

— Every day, he repeated, his voice drowned out, the voice of reason or at least of fact.

— I'd never steal anyone's man, Adele said then. Never. Her face had a tone of weariness when she drank, a weariness that knew the answer to everything. And I'd never break a vow.

— I don't think you would, Phil said.

— I'd never fall for a twenty-year-old, either.

She was talking about the tutor, the girl who had come that time, youth burning through her clothes.

— No, you wouldn't.

— He left his wife, Adele told them.

There was silence.

Phil's bit of smile had gone but his face was still pleasant.

— I didn't leave my wife, he said quietly. She threw me out.

— He left his wife and children, Adele said.

— I didn't leave them. Anyway it was over between us. It had been for more than a year. He said it evenly, almost as if it had happened to someone else. It was my son's tutor, he explained. I fell in love with her.

— And you began something with her? Morrissey suggested.

— Oh, yes.

There is love when you lose the power to speak, when you cannot even breathe.

— Within two or three days, he confessed.

— There in the house?

Phil shook his head. He had a strange, helpless feeling. He was abandoning himself.

— I didn't do anything in the house.

— He left his wife and children, Adele repeated.

8

— You knew that, Phil said.

— Just walked out on them. They'd been married fifteen years, since he was nineteen.

— We hadn't been married fifteen years.

— They had three children, she said, one of them retarded.

Something had happened—he was becoming speechless, he could feel it in his chest like a kind of nausea. As if he were giving up portions of an intimate past.

— He wasn't retarded, he managed to say. He was . . . having trouble learning to read, that's all.

At that instant an aching image of himself and his son from years before came to him. They had rowed one afternoon to the middle of a friend's pond and jumped in, just the two of them. It was summer. His son was six or seven. There was a layer of warm water over deeper, cooler water, the faded green of frogs and weeds. They swam to the far side and then all the way back, the blond head and anxious face of his boy above the surface like a dog's. Year of joy.

— So tell them the rest of it, Adele said.

— There is no rest.

— It turned out this tutor was some kind of call girl. He found her in bed with some guy.

— Is that right? Morrissey said.

He was leaning on the table, his chin in his hand. You think you know someone, you think because you have dinner with them or play cards, but you really don't. It's always a surprise. You know nothing.

— It didn't matter, Phil murmured.

— So stupid marries her anyway, Adele went on. She comes to Mexico City where he's working and he marries her.

— You don't understand anything, Adele, he said.

He wanted to say more but couldn't. It was like being out of breath.

— Do you still talk to her? Morrissey asked casually.

— Yes, over my dead body, Adele said.

None of them could know, none of them could visualize Mexico City and the first unbelievable year, driving down to the coast for the weekend, through Cuernavaca, her bare legs with the sun lying on them, her arms, the dizziness and submission he felt with her as before a forbidden photograph, as if before an overwhelming work of art. Two years in Mexico City oblivious to the wreckage. It was the sense of godliness that empowered him. He could see her neck bent forward with its slender nape. He could see the faint trace of bones like pearls that ran down her smooth back. He could see himself, his former self.

— I talk to her, he admitted.

— And your first wife?

— I talk to her. We have three kids.

— He left her, Adele said. Casanova here.

— Some women have minds like cops, Phil said to no one in particular. This is right, that's wrong. Well, anyway . . .

He stood up. He had done everything wrong, he realized, in the wrong order. He had scuttled his life.

— Anyway there's one thing I can say truthfully. I'd do it all over again if I had the chance.

After he had gone outside they went on talking. The woman whose husband had been unfaithful for seven years knew what it was like.

— He pretends he can't help it, she said. I've had the same thing happen. I was going by Bergdorf's one day and saw a green coat in the window that I liked and I went in and bought it. Then a little while later, someplace else, I saw one that was better than the first one, I thought, so I bought that. Anyway, by the time I was finished I had four green coats hanging in the closet—it was just because I couldn't control my desires.

Outside, the sky, the topmost dome of it, was brushed with clouds and the stars were dim. Adele finally made him out, standing far off in the darkness. She walked unsteadily toward him. His head, she saw, was raised. She stopped a few yards away and raised her head, too. The sky began to whirl. She took an unexpected step or two to steady herself.

— What are you looking at? she finally said.

He did not answer. He had no intention of answering. Then,

— The comet, he said. It's been in the papers. This is the night it's supposed to be most visible.

There was silence.

— I don't see any comet, she said.

— You don't?

— Where is it?

— It's right up there, he gestured. It doesn't look like anything, just like another small star. It's that extra one, by the Pleiades. He knew all the constellations. He had seen them rise in darkness over heartbreaking coasts.

— Come on, you can look at it tomorrow, she said, almost consolingly, though she came no closer to him.

— It won't be there tomorrow. One time only.

— How do you know where it'll be? she said. Come on, it's late, let's get out of here.

He did not move. After a bit she walked toward the house

where, extravagantly, every window upstairs and down was
lit. He stood where he was, looking up at the sky and then at
her as she became smaller and smaller going across the lawn,
reaching first the aura, then the brightness, then tripping on
the kitchen steps.

Eyes of the Stars

S HE WAS SHORT with short legs and her body had lost its
shape. It began at her neck and continued down, and her
arms were like a cook's. In her sixties Teddy had looked the
same for a decade and would probably go on looking the
same, there was not that much to change. She had pouches
under her eyes and a chin, slightly receding when she was a
girl, that was lost now in several others, but she dressed
neatly and people liked her.

Myron, her late husband, had been an ophthalmologist
and proud of the fact that he treated the eyes of many stars,
although frequently it was a relative of a star, a nephew or
mother-in-law, almost the same thing. He could recite the
exact condition of all these eyes, retinitis, mild amblyopia . . .

— So, what is that?

Silvery-haired, he would confide,

—Lazy-eyed.

But Myron was gone. He hadn't really been a very interesting man, Teddy would sometimes admit, apart from knowing
exactly what was wrong with famous patients' eyes. They had

married when she was past forty and resigned to the idea of being single, not that she wouldn't have made a good wife in every way, but she had only her personality and good nature by that time, the rest, as she herself would say, had turned into a size fourteen.

It had not always been that way. Though she did not state, like London's notorious Mrs. Wilson two hundred years earlier, that she would not reveal the circumstances that had made her the mistress of an older man at the age of fifteen, Teddy had had something of the same experience. The first great episode of her life had been with a writer, a detoured novelist more than twenty years older than she was. He had first seen her at a bus stop. She was not, even in those days, exactly beautiful, but there was a body that spoke, at the time, of much that youth could offer. He took her to get her first diaphragm and she was his mistress for three years until he left town and returned to literature and in the end a large house in New Jersey.

She had stayed in touch with him for a time, her real link to the grown-up world, and read his books, of course, but slowly his letters became less frequent until they simply stopped and along with them the foolish hope that he would come back someday.

Through the years she began to remember him less and less as he had been and more as one lone image: driving. The boulevards in those days were wide and very white and the car was weaving a little while he, half-drunk, was telling her stories about actors and parties he had not taken her to.

He had gotten her a job in the story department and she began a long career in the world of movies with its intimate acquaintances, fraudulence, and dreams. One could, though, as that world went, rely on her and she tried to be honest. In the end she became a producer. She had never actually produced anything, but she had suggested things and seen them on the way to realization or oblivion, sometimes both. The marriage to Dr. Hirsch had helped. One of his patients was a rich man who owned a game-show company, and through him she met figures in television. It was after she was widowed that the long-awaited opportunity came. She was invited to coproduce a show that turned out to be a success, and a year later she became the sole producer when her partner fell in love and left to marry a Venezuelan businessman. Easygoing in manner, sentimental but shrewd, she drove to work in an inexpensive car and was well liked by the crew. They wanted to please her, to see her laugh and smile.

YOU WILL PROBABLY RECOGNIZE the outlines of the plot. A romantic and mysterious figure, cynical and well able to take care of himself, is, beneath all that, a lost idealist. In this version he is a lawyer, first in his class at law school, who throws it all in after several years in a large firm and proceeds on his own, as much investigator as anything else and not above fixing a DUI charge for a suitable fee. In short, the dark hero of dime novels. In one memorable episode he leaves the office in evening clothes to drive to a birthday party in Palm Springs where he sees the moral rot of his rich client and ends up seducing the wife.

The fortunate thing was how well the actor fit the role. Boothman Keck was in his forties but looked younger. He had come late to acting, taking his twelve-year-old son to an open call one afternoon and being asked if he had ever done any acting himself.

— No, he said.

— None? Never?

— Well, not that I know of.

He had a quality they were seeking for a small part as an alcoholic who still had an essential manhood.

— So, what do you do for a living?

— I'm a swimming coach, Keck said.

— Personal?

— No, I coach a team. A high school team, he explained.

They liked him. Luck followed. The movie got some attention and he with it. Teddy had hired him. He was not impressed with her at first, but over time he began to see her differently and even to like her looks, the fact that she was heavy, that she was short. For some reason she called him Bud. They got along. He had had an ordinary life but was now living one that was the complete opposite. He never lost his modesty.

— It's all a dream, he would admit.

Then Deborah Legley, who had not been in a movie for some years but whose name was still alive—the slender arrogance when she was younger, the marriage to an immortal— came from the east for a guest appearance. She was being paid a lot of money, too much, Teddy felt, and from the beginning she was difficult. She came off the plane in dark glasses and no makeup though expecting to be recognized. Teddy met her on arrival. They had to wait a little too long for the car. On the set she turned out to be a monster. She made everyone wait, snubbed the director, and barely acknowledged the presence of the crew.

Teddy had to invite her to dinner and invited Keck, too, whose wife was out of town, to make the evening bearable. She bought caviar, Beluga, in the large round tin with the sturgeon on the label. She set the caviar in crushed ice with lemon halves around it. They would have caviar, a drink, and go on to the restaurant. Keck was picking up Deborah at the hotel. Teddy looked at her watch. It was past seven. They would arrive before long.

PARKING BENEATH the tall black palms, Keck went into the hotel and up to the suite. A dog began to bark when he knocked. He waited and then knocked again. He stood looking at the carpet. Finally,

— Who is it?

— It's Booth.

— Who?

— Booth, he said loudly.

— Just a minute.

An equally long time passed. The dog had stopped barking. There was silence. He knocked again. At last, like the sweeping aside of a great curtain, the door opened.

— Come in, she said. I'm sorry, were you waiting?

She was wearing a tan silk jacket, casual in a way, and a smooth white T-shirt beneath.

— Something spilled in the bathroom, she explained, fastening an earring and preceding him into the room. Anyway, this ghastly dinner. What are we going to do?

17

The dog was sniffing his leg.

— The thought of spending the evening with that boring woman, she went on, is more than I can bear. I don't know how you put up with her. Here, sit.

She patted the couch beside her. The dog leapt onto it.

— Get down, Sammy, she said, pushing him with the back of her hand.

She patted the couch again.

— She's an idiot. That driver at the airport had a big sign with my name on it, can you imagine? Put that down, I told him.

Her nostrils flared in annoyance or anger, Keck could not tell. She had two distinct ways of doing it. One was in pride and anger, a thoroughbred flaring. The other was more intimate, like the raising of an eyebrow.

— The stupidity! He wanted to wave it around so people could see it, make himself important. Exactly what one needs, isn't it? If there'd been anything, the least little thing wrong here at the hotel, I'd have flown straight back to New York. Bye-bye. But of course, they know me here, I've been here so many times.

— I guess so.

— So, what are we going to do? she said. Let's have a drink and figure something out. There's white wine in the fridge. I only drink white wine now. Is that all right for you? We can order something.

— I don't think we have enough time, Keck said.

— We have plenty of time.

The dog had gripped Keck's leg with its own two front legs.

— Sammy, she said, stop.

Keck tried to disengage himself.

— Later, Sammy, he said.

— He seems to like you, she said. But then who wouldn't, hm? You have your car, don't you? Why don't we just drive down to Santa Monica and have dinner?

— You mean, without Teddy?

— Completely without her.

— We should call her.

— Darling, that's for you, she said in a warm voice.

Keck sat down by the phone, uncertain of what to say.

— Hello, Teddy? It's Booth. No, I'm at the hotel, he said. Listen, Deborah's dog is sick. She isn't going to be able to come to dinner. We'll have to call it off.

— Her dog? What's wrong with it? Teddy said.

— Oh, it's been throwing up and it can't . . . it's having trouble walking.

— She's probably looking for a vet. I have a good one. Hold on, I'll get the number.

— No that's all right, Keck said. One is already coming. She got him through the hotel.

— Well, tell her I'm sorry. If you need the other number, call me.

When he hung up, Keck said,

— It's OK.

— You lie almost as well as I do.

She poured some wine.

— Or would you rather have something else? she said again. We can drink here or we can drink there.

— Where's that?

— Do you know Rank's? It's down off Pacific. I haven't been there in ages.

It was not quite night. The sky was an intense, deep blue,

vast and cloudless. She sat beside him as they headed for the beach, her graceful neck, her cheeks, her perfume. He felt like an imposter. She still represented beauty. Her body seemed youthful. How old was she? Fifty-five, at least, but with barely a wrinkle. A goddess still. It would have once been beyond imagination to think of driving down Wilshire with her toward the last of the light.

— You don't smoke, do you? she said.

— No.

— Good. I hate cigarettes. Nick smoked day and night. Of course, it killed him. That's something you never want to see, when it spreads to the bone and nothing stops the pain. It's horrible. Here we are.

There was a blue neon sign from which the first letter—F— was gone; it had been gone for years. Inside it was noisy and dark.

— Is Frank here? Deborah asked the waiter.

— Just a minute, he said. I'll go and see.

Some heads had turned when she walked past the bar, her insolent walk and then seeing who she was. After a few minutes a young man in a shirt without a tie came back to where they were sitting.

— You were asking for Frank? he said, recognizing them but politely not showing it. Frank isn't here anymore.

— What happened? Deborah said.

— He sold the place.

— When was that?

— A year and a half ago.

Deborah nodded.

— You ought to change the name or something, she said, so you don't fool people.

— Well, it's always been the name of the place. We have the same menu, the same chef, he explained cordially.

— Good for you, she said. Then to Keck, Let's go.

— Did I say something wrong? the new owner asked.

— Probably, she said.

TEDDY HAD CALLED and cancelled the reservation. She wondered about the dog. She hadn't bothered to remember its name. It had lain in its bed on the set, head on paws, watching. Teddy had had a dog for years, an English pug named Ava, all wrinkled velvet with bulging eyes and a comic nature. Deaf and nearly blind at the end, unable to walk, she was carried into the garden four or five times a day where she stood on trembling legs and looked up at Teddy helplessly with chalky, unseeing eyes. At last there was nothing that could be done and Teddy drove her to the vet for the last time. She carried her in, tears running down her cheeks. The vet pretended not to notice. He greeted the old dog instead.

— Hello, princess, he said gently.

With one of the small ivory spoons Teddy put some caviar on a piece of toast and ate it. She went into the kitchen for the chopped egg and brought it into the living room. She decided to have some vodka as well. There was a bottle of it in the freezer.

With the egg and a squeeze of lemon she served herself more caviar. There was far too much of it to even think of eating; she would bring it to the set the next day, she decided. There were only two more weeks of shooting. Perhaps she would take a short vacation afterward. She might go down to Baja where some friends were going. She had been to Baja when she was sixteen. You were able to drink in Mexico and do anything, although by that time they were often in separate beds. They had twin beds in the apartment on Venice Boulevard and also that summer in Malibu in a house rented from an actor who had gone on location for six weeks. There was a leafy passageway that led to the beach. She didn't wear a bikini that summer, she was too embarrassed to, she remembered. She had a one-piece black bathing suit, the same one every day, and an abortion that fall.

THERE WAS A MOTH on the windshield as they headed back. They were going forty miles an hour; its wings were quivering in what must have been a titanic wind as it resisted being borne into the night. Still, stubbornly, it clung, like gray ash but thick and trembling.

— What are you doing? she said.

Keck had pulled over and stopped. He reached out and pushed the moth a little. Abruptly it flew into the darkness.

— Are you a Buddhist or something?

— No, he said. I didn't know if it wanted to go where we're going, that's all.

At Jack's they were quickly given a good table. She had come here all the time when she lived out here and was making movies, she said.

— I've seen all of them, Keck said.

— Well, you should have. They were good. But you were a little kid. How old are you?

— Forty-three.

— Forty-three. Not bad, she said.

— I won't ask you.

— Don't be crass, she warned.

— Whatever it is, you don't look it. You look about thirty.

— Thank you.

— I mean, it's astonishing.

— Don't let it be too astonishing.

What was her accent, was it English or just languid upper-class? It was different in those days, she was saying. That was when there were geniuses, great directors, Huston, Billy Wilder, Hitch. You learned a lot from them.

— You know why? she said. Because they had actually lived, they just didn't grow up on movies. They'd been in the war.

— Hitchcock?

— Huston, Ford.

— How did you and Nick meet? Keck asked.

— He saw a photo of me, she said.

— Is that the truth?

— In a white bathing suit. No, somebody made that up. They make up all kinds of things. We met at a party at the Bistro. I was eighteen. He asked me to dance. Somehow I lost an earring and was looking for it. He'd find it, he said, call him the next day. Well, you can imagine, he was one of the god kings, it was pretty heady stuff. Anyway, I called. He said to come to his house.

Keck could see it, eighteen and more or less innocent, everything still ahead of her. If she took off her clothes you would never forget it.

— So, you did.

— When I got there, she said, he had a bottle of champagne and the bed turned down.

23

— So that was it?

— Not quite, she said.

— What happened?

— I told him, thanks, just the earring, please.

— That's the truth?

— Look, he was forty-five, I was eighteen. I mean, let's see what's going on. Let's not raise the curtain so fast.

— The curtain?

— You know what I mean. He'd been quite the ladies' man. I took care of that, she said.

She looked at him with knowing eyes.

— You men get all excited by young girls. You think they're some kind of erotic toy. You haven't met a real woman, that's the difference.

— The difference.

Her nostrils flared.

— With a real woman, the buck stops here, she said.

— I don't know what that means.

— You don't, eh? I think you do.

After a while, she said,

— So, where is your wife this evening?

— Vancouver. She's visiting her sister.

— All the way up in Vancouver.

— Yeah.

— That's a long way from here. You know one of the things I've learned? she said.

— No, what?

— One never has the human company one longs for. Something else is always offered.

Perhaps it was a line from a play.

— Like me, you mean?

— No, sweetheart, not like you. At least I don't think so.

He felt uneasy. *What's wrong, are you afraid of something?* she was going to say. *No, why? You're acting afraid.*

There was a knot in his stomach. *What is it, your wife?* she was going to ask. *Oh, yes, I forgot, the wife. There's always the wife.*

Deborah had gone to the ladies' room.

— Hello, Teddy? Keck said. He was talking on his cell phone. I just thought I'd call you.

— Where are you? What's happened? Is the dog all right?

— Yeah, the dog's OK. We're at a restaurant.

— Well, it's a little late . . .

— Don't you even budge. I'm taking care of it. I'll handle it.

— Is she behaving?

— This woman? Let me tell you something: it's even worse if she likes you.

— What do you mean?

— I can't talk anymore, I see her coming back. You're lucky you're not here.

TEDDY, having hung up the phone, sat by herself. The vodka had left her with a pleasant feeling and the disinclination to wonder where the two of them were. The chair was comfortable. The garden, through the French doors, was dark. She was not thinking of anything in particular. She looked around at the familiar furniture, the flowers, the lamplight. She found herself, for some reason, thinking about her life, a thing she did not do often. She had a nice house, not large but perfect for her. You could even, from a place on the lawn, see a bit of the ocean. There was a maid's room and a guest room, the closet in the latter filled with her clothes. She had difficulty throwing things away and there were clothes for any occasion, though the occasion may have been long past. Still, she did not like to think of beautifully made things in the trash. But there was no one to give them to, the maid had no use for them, there was no one who would even wear them.

The years of her marriage, looking back, had been good ones. Myron Hirsch had left her with more than enough to take care of herself, and the success she had had was on top of that. For a woman of few talents—was that true? perhaps she was shortchanging herself—she had done pretty well. She was remembering how it had started. She remembered the beer bottles rolling around in the back of the car when she was fifteen and he was making love to her every morning and she did not know if she was beginning life or throwing it away, but she loved him and would never forget.

My Lord You

———◆———

THERE WERE CRUMPLED NAPKINS on the table, wine-glasses still with dark remnant in them, coffee stains, and plates with bits of hardened Brie. Beyond the bluish windows the garden lay motionless beneath the birdsong of summer morning. Daylight had come. It had been a success except for one thing: Brennan.

They had sat around first, drinking in the twilight, and then gone inside. The kitchen had a large round table, fire-place, and shelves with ingredients of every kind. Deems was well known as a cook. So was his somewhat unknowable girl-friend, Irene, who had a mysterious smile though they never cooked together. That night it was Deems's turn. He served caviar, brought out in a white jar such as makeup comes in, to be eaten from small silver spoons.

— The only way, Deems muttered in profile. He seldom looked at anyone. Antique silver spoons, Ardis heard him mistakenly say in his low voice, as if it might not have been noticed.

She was noticing everything, however. Though they had

known Deems for a while, she and her husband had never been to the house. In the dining room, when they all went in to dinner, she took in the pictures, books, and shelves of objects including one of perfect, gleaming shells. It was foreign in a way, like anyone else's house, but half-familiar.

There'd been some mix-up about the seating that Irene tried vainly to adjust amid the conversation before the meal began. Outside, darkness had come, deep and green. The men were talking about camps they had gone to as boys in piny Maine and about Soros, the financier. Far more interesting was a comment Ardis heard Irene make, in what context she did not know,

— I think there's such a thing as sleeping with one man too many.

— Did you say "such a thing" or "no such thing"? she heard herself ask.

Irene merely smiled. I must ask her later, Ardis thought. The food was excellent. There was cold soup, duck, and a salad of young vegetables. The coffee had been served and Ardis was distractedly playing with melted wax from the candles when a voice burst out loudly behind her,

— I'm late. Who's this? Are these the beautiful people?

It was a drunken man in a jacket and dirty white trousers with blood on them, which had come from nicking his lip while shaving two hours before. His hair was damp, his face arrogant. It was the face of a Regency duke, intimidating, spoiled. The irrational flickered from him.

— Do you have anything to drink here? What is this, wine? Very sorry I'm late. I've just had seven cognacs and said goodbye to my wife. Deems, you know what that's like. You're my only friend, do you know that? The only one.

— There's some dinner in there, if you like, Deems said, gesturing toward the kitchen.

— No dinner. I've had dinner. I'll just have something to drink. Deems, you're my friend, but I'll tell you something, you'll become my enemy. You know what Oscar Wilde said— my favorite writer, my favorite in all the world. Anyone can choose his friends, but only the wise man can choose his enemies.

He was staring intently at Deems. It was like the grip of a madman, a kind of fury. His mouth had an expression of determination. When he went into the kitchen they could hear him among the bottles. He returned with a dangerous glassful and looked around boldly.

— Where is Beatrice? Deems asked.

— Who?

— Beatrice, your wife.

— Gone, Brennan said.

He searched for a chair.

— To visit her father? Irene asked.

— What makes you think that? Brennan said menacingly. To Ardis's alarm he sat down next to her.

— He's been in the hospital, hasn't he?

— Who knows where he's been, Brennan said darkly. He's a swine. Lucre, gain. He's a slum owner, a criminal. I would hang him myself. In the fashion of Gomez, the dictator, whose daughters are probably wealthy women.

He discovered Ardis and said to her, as if imitating someone, perhaps someone he assumed her to be,

— 'N 'at funny? 'N 'at wonderful?

To her relief he turned away.

— I'm their only hope, he said to Irene. I'm living on their

29

money and it's ruinous, the end of me. He held out his glass and asked mildly, Can I have just a tiny bit of ice? I adore my wife. To Ardis he confided, Do you know how we met? Unimaginable. She was walking by on the beach. I was unprepared. I saw the ventral, then the dorsal, I imagined the rest. Bang! We came together like planets. Endless fornication. Sometimes I just lie silent and observe her. *The black panther lies under his rose-tree*, he recited. *J'ai eu pitié des autres* . . .

He stared at her.

— What is that? she asked tentatively.

— . . . *but that the child walk in peace in her basilica*, he intoned.

— Is it Wilde?

— You can't guess? Pound. The sole genius of the century. No, not the sole. I am another: a drunk, a failure, and a great genius. Who are you? he said. Another little housewife?

She felt the blood leave her face and stood to busy herself clearing the table. His hand was on her arm.

— Don't go. I know who you are, another priceless woman meant to languish. Beautiful figure, he said as she managed to free herself, pretty shoes.

As she carried some plates into the kitchen she could hear him saying,

— Don't go to many of these parties. Not invited.

— Can't imagine why, someone murmured.

— But Deems is my friend, my very closest friend.

— Who is he? Ardis asked Irene in the kitchen.

— Oh, he's a poet. He's married to a Venezuelan woman and she runs off. He's not always this bad.

They had quieted him down in the other room. Ardis could

see her husband nervously pushing his glasses up on his nose with one finger. Deems, in a polo shirt and with rumpled hair, was trying to guide Brennan toward the back door. Brennan kept stopping to talk. For a moment he would seem reformed.

—I want to tell you something, he said. I went past the school, the one on the street there. There was a poster. The First Annual Miss Fuck Contest. I'm serious. This is a fact.

— No, no, Deems said.

— It's been held, I don't know when. Question is, are they coming to their senses finally or losing them? A tiny bit more, he begged; his glass was empty. His mind doubled back, Seriously, what do you think of that?

In the light of the kitchen he seemed merely dishevelled, like a journalist who has been working hard all night. The unsettling thing was the absence of reason in him, his glare. One nostril was smaller than the other. He was used to being ungovernable. Ardis hoped he would not notice her again. His forehead had two gleaming places, like nascent horns. Were men drawn to you when they knew they were frightening you?

She could feel his eyes. There was silence. She could feel him standing there like a menacing beggar.

— What are you, another bourgeois? he said to her. I know I've been drinking. Come and have dinner, he said. I've ordered something wonderful for us. Vichyssoise. Lobster. S. G. Always on the menu like that, *selon grosseur.*

He was talking in an easy way, as if they were in the casino together, chips piled high before them, as if it were a shrewd discussion of what to bet on and her breasts in the dark

T-shirt were a thing of indifference to him. He calmly reached out and touched one.

— I have money, he said. His hand remained where it was, cupping her. She was too stunned to move. Do you want me to do more of that?

— No, she managed to say.

His hand slipped down to her hip. Deems had taken an arm and was drawing him away.

— Ssh, Brennan whispered to her, don't say anything, The two of us. Like an oar going into the water, gliding.

— We have to go, Deems insisted.

— What are you doing? Is this another of your ruses? Brennan cried. Deems, I shall end up destroying you yet!

As he was herded to the door, he continued. Deems was the only man he didn't loathe, he said. He wanted them all to come to his house, he had everything. He had a phonograph, whisky! He had a gold watch!

At last he was outside. He walked unsteadily across the finely cut grass and got into his car, the side of which was dented in. He backed away in great lurches.

— He's headed for Cato's, Deems guessed. I ought to call and warn them.

— They won't serve him. He owes them money, Irene said.

— Who told you that?

— The bartender. Are you all right? she asked Ardis.

— Yes. Is he actually married?

— He's been married three or four times, Deems said.

Later they started dancing, some of the women together. Irene pulled Deems onto the floor. He came unresisting. He danced quite well. She was moving her arms sinuously and singing.

— Very nice, he said. Have you ever entertained?

She smiled at him.

— I do my best, she said.

At the end she put her hand on Ardis's arm and said again,

— I'm so embarrassed at what happened.

— It was nothing. I'm all right.

— I should have taken him and thrown him out, her husband said on the way home. Ezra Pound. Do you know about Ezra Pound?

— No.

— He was a traitor. He broadcast for the enemy during the war. They should have shot him.

— What happened to him?

— They gave him a poetry prize.

They were going down a long empty stretch where on a corner, half hidden in trees, a small house stood, the gypsy house, Ardis thought of it as, a simple house with a water pump in the yard and occasionally in the daytime a girl in blue shorts, very brief, and high heels, hanging clothes on a line. Tonight there was a light on in the window. One light near the sea. She was driving with Warren and he was talking.

— The best thing is to just forget about tonight.

— Yes, she said. It was nothing.

Brennan went through a fence on Hull Lane and up on to somebody's lawn at about two that morning. He had missed the curve where the road bent left, probably because his headlights weren't on, the police thought.

SHE TOOK THE BOOK and went over to a window that looked out on the garden behind the library. She read a bit of one

33

thing or another and came to a poem some lines of which had been underlined, with pencilled notes in the margin. It was "The River-Merchant's Wife"; she had never heard of it. Outside, the summer burned, white as chalk.

At fourteen I married My Lord you, she read.
I never laughed, being bashful . . .

There were three old men, one of them almost blind, it appeared, reading newspapers in the cold room. The thick glasses of the nearly blind man cast white moons onto his cheeks.

The leaves fall early this autumn, in wind.
The paired butterflies are already yellow with August
Over the grass in the West garden;
They hurt me. I grow older.

She had read poems and perhaps marked them like this, but that was in school. Of the things she had been taught she remembered only a few. There had been one My Lord though she did not marry him. She'd been twenty-one, her first year in the city. She remembered the building of dark brown brick on Fifty-eighth Street, the afternoons with their slitted light, her clothes in a chair or fallen to the floor, and the damp, mindless repetition, to it, or him, or who knew what: oh, God, oh, God, oh, God. The traffic outside so faint, so far away . . .

She'd called him several times over the years, believing that love never died, dreaming foolishly of seeing him again, of his returning, in the way of old songs. To hurry, to almost run down the noontime street again, the sound of

34

her heels on the sidewalk. To see the door of the apartment open . . .

> *If you are coming down the narrows of the river Kiang,*
> *Please let me know beforehand,*
> *And I will come out to meet you.*
> *As far as Chô-fu-Sa*

There she sat by the window with her young face that had a weariness in it, a slight distaste for things, even, one might imagine for oneself. After a while she went to the desk.

— Do you happen to have anything by Michael Brennan? she asked.

— Michael Brennan, the woman said. We've had them, but he takes them away because unworthy people read them, he says. I don't think there're any now. Perhaps when he comes back from the city.

— He lives in the city?

— He lives just down the road. We had all of his books at one time. Do you know him?

She would have liked to ask more but she shook her head.

— No, she said. I've just heard the name.

— He's a poet, the woman said.

ON THE BEACH she sat by herself. There was almost no one. In her bathing suit she lay back with the sun on her face and knees. It was hot and the sea calm. She preferred to lie up by the dunes with the waves bursting, to listen while they crashed like the final chords of a symphony except they went on and on. There was nothing as fine as that.

35

She came out of the ocean and dried herself like the gypsy girl, ankles caked with sand. She could feel the sun burnishing her shoulders. Hair wet, deep in the emptiness of days, she walked her bicycle up to the road, the dirt velvety beneath her feet.

She did not go home the usual way. There was little traffic. The noon was bottle-green, large houses among the trees and wide farmland, like a memory, behind.

She knew the house and saw it far off, her heart beating strangely. When she stopped, it was casually, with the bike tilting to one side and she half-seated on it as if taking a rest. How beautiful a lone woman is, in a white summer shirt and bare legs. Pretending to adjust the bicycle's chain she looked at the house, its tall windows, water stains high on the roof. There was a gardener's shed, abandoned, saplings growing in the path that led to it. The long driveway, the sea porch, everything was empty.

Walking slowly, aware of how brazen she was, she went toward the house. Her urge was to look in the windows, no more than that. Still, despite the silence, the complete stillness, that was forbidden.

She walked farther. Suddenly someone rose from the side porch. She was unable to utter a sound or move.

It was a dog, a huge dog higher than her waist, coming toward her, yellow-eyed. She had always been afraid of dogs, the Alsatian that had unexpectedly turned on her college roommate and torn off a piece of her scalp. The size of this one, its lowered head and slow, deliberate stride.

Do not show fear, she knew that. Carefully she moved the bicycle so that it was between them. The dog stopped a few feet away, its eyes directly on her, the sun along its back. She did not know what to expect, a sudden short rush.

— Good boy, she said. It was all she could think of. Good boy.

Moving cautiously, she began wheeling the bicycle toward the road, turning her head away slightly so as to appear unworried. Her legs felt naked, the bare calves. They would be ripped open as if by a scythe. The dog was following her, its shoulders moving smoothly, like a kind of machine. Somehow finding the courage, she tried to ride. The front wheel wavered. The dog, high as the handlebars, came nearer.

— No, she cried. No!

After a moment or two, obediently, he slowed or veered off. He was gone.

She rode as if freed, as if flying through blocks of sunlight and high, solemn tunnels of trees. And then she saw him again. He was following—not exactly following, since he was some distance ahead. He seemed to float along in the fields, which were burning in the midday sun, on fire. She turned onto her own road. There he came. He fell in behind her. She could hear the clatter of his nails like falling stones. She looked back. He was trotting awkwardly, like a big man running in the rain. A line of spittle trailed from his jaw. When she reached her house he had disappeared.

THAT NIGHT in a cotton robe she was preparing for bed, cleaning her face, the bathroom door ajar. She brushed her hair with many rapid strokes.

— Tired? her husband asked as she emerged.

It was his way of introducing the subject.

— No, she said.

So there they were in the summer night with the far-off sound of the sea. Among the things her husband admired that Ardis possessed was extraordinary skin, luminous and smooth, a skin so pure that to touch it would make one tremble.

— Wait, she whispered, —not so fast.

Afterward he lay back without a word, already falling into deepest sleep, much too soon. She touched his shoulder. She heard something outside the window.

— Did you hear that?

— No, what? he said drowsily.

She waited. There was nothing. It had seemed faint, like a sigh.

The next morning she said,

— Oh! There, just beneath the trees, the dog lay. She could see his ears—they were small ears dashed with white.

— What is it? her husband asked.

— Nothing, she said. A dog. It followed me yesterday.

— From where? he said, coming to see.

— Down the road. I think it might be that man's. Brennan's.

— Brennan?

— I passed his house, she said, and afterward it was following me.

— What were you doing at Brennan's?

— Nothing. I was passing. He's not even there.

— What do you mean, he's not there?

— I don't know. Somebody said that.

He went to the door and opened it. The dog—it was a

deerhound—had been lying with its forelegs stretched out in front like a sphinx, its haunches round and high. Awkwardly it rose and after a moment moved, reluctantly it seemed, wandering slowly across the fields, never looking back.

In the evening they went to a party on Mecox Road. Far out toward Montauk, winds were sweeping the coast. The waves exploded in clouds of spray. Ardis was talking to a woman not much older than herself, whose husband had just died of a brain tumor at the age of forty. He had diagnosed it himself, the woman said. He'd been sitting in a theater when he suddenly realized he couldn't see the wall just to his right. At the funeral, she said, there had been two women she did not recognize and who did not come to the reception afterward.

— Of course, he was a surgeon, she said, and they're drawn to surgeons like flies. But I never suspected. I suppose I'm the world's greatest fool.

The trees streamed past in the dark as they drove home. Their house rose in the brilliant headlights. She thought she had caught sight of something and found herself hoping her husband had not. She was nervous as they walked across the grass. The stars were numberless. They would open the door and go inside, where all was familiar, even serene.

After a while they would prepare for bed while the wind seized the corners of the house and the dark leaves thrashed each other. They would turn out the lights. All that was outside would be left in wildness, in the glory of the wind.

IT WAS TRUE. He was there. He was lying on his side, his whitish coat ruffled. In the morning light she approached slowly. When he raised his head his eyes were hazel and gold.

He was not that young, she saw, but his power was that he was unbowed. She spoke in a natural voice.

— Come, she said.

She took a few steps. At first he did not move. She glanced back again. He was following.

It was still early. As they reached the road a car passed, drab and sun-faded. A girl was in the back seat, head fallen wearily, being driven home, Ardis thought, after the exhausting night. She felt an inexplicable envy.

It was warm but the true heat had not risen. Several times she waited while he drank from puddles at the edge of the road, standing in them as he did, his large, wet toenails gleaming like ivory.

Suddenly from a porch rushed another dog, barking fiercely. The great hound turned, teeth bared. She held her breath, afraid of the sight of one of them limp and bleeding, but violent as it sounded they kept a distance between them. After a few snaps it was over. He came along less steadily, strands of wet hair near his mouth.

At the house he went to the porch and stood waiting. It was plain he wanted to go inside. He had returned. He must be starving, she thought. She looked around to see if there was anyone in sight. A chair she had not noticed before was out on the grass, but the house was as still as ever, not even the curtains breathing. With a hand that seemed not even hers she tried the door. It was unlocked.

The hallway was dim. Beyond it was a living room in disorder, couch cushions rumpled, glasses on the tables, papers, shoes. In the dining room there were piles of books. It was the house of an artist, abundance, disregard.

There was a large desk in the bedroom, in the middle of which, among paper clips and letters, a space had been cleared. Here were sheets of paper written in an almost illegible hand, incomplete lines and words that omitted certain vowels. *Deth of fathr,* she read, then indecipherable things and something that seemed to be *carrges sent empty,* and at the bottom, set apart, two words, *anew, anew.* In a different hand was the page of a letter, *I deeply love you. I admire you. I love you and admire you.* She could not read anymore. She was too uneasy. There were things she did not want to know. In a hammered silver frame was the photograph of a woman, face darkened by shadow, leaning against a wall, the unseen white of a villa somewhere behind. Through the slatted blinds one could hear the soft clack of palm fronds, the birds high above, in the villa where he had found her, where her youth had been bold as a declaration of war. No, that was not it. He had met her on a beach, they had gone to the villa. What is powerful is a glimpse of a truer life. She read the slanting inscription in Spanish, *Tus besos me destierran.* She put the picture down. A photograph was sacrosanct, you were excluded from it, always. So that was the wife. *Tus besos,* your kisses.

SHE WANDERED, nearly dreaming, into a large bathroom that looked out on the garden. As she entered, her heart almost stopped—she caught sight of somebody in the mirror. It took a second before she realized it was herself and, as she looked more closely, a not wholly recognizable, even an illicit self, in soft, grainy light. She understood suddenly, she accepted the fate that meant she was to be found here, that

Brennan would be returning and discover her, having stopped for the mail or bread. Out of nowhere she would hear the paralyzing sound of footsteps or a car. Still, she continued to look at herself. She was in the house of the poet, the demon. She had entered forbidden rooms. *Tus besos* . . . the words had not died. At that moment the dog came to the door, stood there, and then fell to the floor, his knowing eyes on her, like an intimate friend. She turned to him. All she had never done seemed at hand.

Deliberately, without thinking, she began to remove her clothes. She went no further than the waist. She was dazzled by what she was doing. There in the silence with the sunlight outside she stood slender and half-naked, the missing image of herself, of all women. The dog's eyes were raised to her as if in reverence. He was unbetraying, a companion like no other. She remembered certain figures ahead of her at school. Kit Vining, Nan Boudreau. Legendary faces and reputations. She had longed to be like them but never seemed to have the chance. She leaned forward to stroke the beautiful head.

— You're a big fellow. The words seemed authentic, more authentic than anything she had said for a long time. A very big fellow.

His long tail stirred and with faint sound brushed the floor. She kneeled and stroked his head again and again.

There was the crackling of gravel beneath the tires of a car. It brought her abruptly to her senses. Hurriedly, almost in panic, she threw on her clothes and made her way to the kitchen. She would run along the porch if necessary and then from tree to tree.

She opened the door and listened. Nothing. As she was

going quickly down the back steps, by the side of the house she saw her husband. Thank God, she thought helplessly.

They approached each other slowly. He glanced at the house.

— I brought the car. Is anyone here?

There was a moment's pause.

— No, no one. She felt her face stiffen, as if she were telling a lie.

— What were you doing? he asked.

— I was in the kitchen, she said. I was trying to find something to feed him.

— Did you find it?

— Yes. No, she said.

He stood looking at her and finally said,

— Let's go.

As they backed out, she caught sight of the dog just lying down in the shade, sprawled, disconsolate. She felt the nakedness beneath her clothes, the satisfaction. They turned onto the road.

— Somebody's got to feed him, she said as they drove. She was looking out at the houses and fields. Warren said nothing. He was driving faster. She turned back to look. For a moment she thought she saw him following, far behind.

LATE THAT DAY she went shopping and came home about five. The wind, which had arisen anew, blew the door shut with a bang.

— Warren?

— Did you see him? her husband said.

— Yes.

He had come back. He was out there where the land went up slightly.

— I'm going to call the animal shelter, she said.

— They won't do anything. He's not a stray.

— I can't stand it. I'm calling someone, she said.

— Why don't you call the police? Maybe they'll shoot him.

— Why don't you do it? she said coldly. Borrow someone's gun. He's driving me crazy.

It remained light until past nine, and in the last of it, with the clouds a deeper blue than the sky, she went out quietly, far across the grass. Her husband watched from the window. She was carrying a white bowl.

She could see him very clearly, the gray of his muzzle there in the muted grass and when she was close the clear, tan eyes. In an almost ceremonial way she knelt down. The wind was blowing her hair. She seemed almost a mad person there in the fading light.

— Here. Drink something, she said.

His gaze, somehow reproachful, drifted away. He was like a fugitive sleeping on his coat. His eyes were nearly closed.

My life has meant nothing, she thought. She wanted above all else not to confess that.

They ate dinner in silence. Her husband did not look at her. Her face annoyed him, he did not know why. She could be good-looking but there were times when she was not. Her face was like a series of photographs, some of which ought to have been thrown away. Tonight it was like that.

— The sea broke through into Sag Pond today, she said dully.

— Did it?

— They thought some little girl had drowned. The fire

trucks were there. It turned out she had just strayed off. After a pause, We have to do something, she said.

— Whatever happens is going to happen, he told her.

— This is different, she said. She suddenly left the room. She felt close to tears.

Her husband's business was essentially one of giving advice. He had a life that served other lives, helped them come to agreements, end marriages, defend themselves against former friends. He was accomplished at it. Its language and techniques were part of him. He lived amid disturbance and self-interest but always protected from it. In his files were letters, memorandums, secrets of careers. One thing he had seen: how near men could be to disaster no matter how secure they seemed. He had seen events turn, one ruinous thing following another. It could happen without warning. Sometimes they were able to save themselves, but there was a point at which they could not. He sometimes wondered about himself—when the blow came and the beams began to give and come apart, what would happen? She was calling Brennan's house again. There was never an answer.

During the night the wind blew itself out. In the morning at first light, Warren could feel the stillness. He lay in bed without moving. His wife's back was turned toward him. He could feel her denial.

He rose and went to the window. The dog was still there, he could see its shape. He knew little of animals and nothing of nature but he could tell what had happened. It was lying in a different way.

— What is it? she asked. She had come up beside him. It seemed she stood there for a long time. He's dead.

She started for the door. He held her by the arm.

— Let me go, she said.

— Ardis . . .

She began to weep,

— Let me go.

— Leave him alone! he called after her. Let him be!

She ran quickly across the grass in her nightgown. The ground was wet. As she came closer she paused to calm herself, to find courage. She regretted only one thing—she had not said good-bye.

She took a step or two forward. She could sense the heavy, limp weight of him, a weight that would disperse, become something else, the sinews fading, the bones becoming light. She longed to do what she had never done, embrace him. At that moment he raised his head.

— Warren! she cried, turning toward the house. Warren!

As if the shouts distressed him, the dog was rising to his feet. He moved wearily off. Hands pressed to her mouth, she stared at the place where he had been, where the grass was flattened slightly. All night again. Again all night. When she looked, he was some distance off.

She ran after him. Warren could see her. She seemed free. She seemed like another woman, a younger woman, the kind one saw in the dusty fields by the sea, in a bikini, stealing potatoes in bare feet.

SHE DID NOT see him again. She went many times past the house, occasionally seeing Brennan's car there, but never a sign of the dog, or along the road or off in the fields.

One night in Cato's at the end of August, she saw Brennan

himself at the bar. His arm was in a sling, from what sort of accident she could not guess. He was talking intently to the bartender, the same fierce eloquence, and though the restaurant was crowded, the stools next to him were empty. He was alone. The dog was not outside, nor in his car, nor part of his life anymore—gone, lost, living elsewhere, his name perhaps to be written in a line someday though most probably he was forgotten, but not by her.

Such Fun

———◆———

WHEN THEY LEFT the restaurant, Leslie wanted to go and have a drink at her place, it was only a few blocks away, a large old apartment building with leaded windows on the ground floor and a view over Washington Square. Kathrin said fine, but Jane claimed she was tired.

— Just one drink, Leslie said. Come on.

— It's too early to go home, Kathrin added.

In the restaurant they had talked about movies, ones they'd seen and ones they hadn't. They talked about movies and Rudy, the headwaiter.

— I always get one of the good tables, said Leslie.

— Is that right?

— Always.

— And what does he get?

— It's what he hopes he'll get, Leslie said.

— He's really looking at Jane.

— No, he's not, Jane protested.

— He's got half your clothes off already.

— Don't, please, Jane said.

Leslie and Kathrin had been roommates in college and friends ever since. They had hitchhiked through Europe together, getting as far as Turkey, sleeping in the same bed a lot of the nights and, except once, not fooling around with men or, as it happened that time, boys. Kathrin had long hair combed back dark from a handsome brow and a brilliant smile. She could easily have been a model. There was not much more to her than met the eye, but that had always been enough. Leslie had majored in music but hadn't done anything with it. She had a wonderful way on the telephone, as if she'd known you for years.

In the elevator, Kathrin said,

— God, he's cute.

— Who?

— Your doorman. What's his name?

— Santos. He's from Colombia someplace.

— What time does he get off is what I want to know.

— For God's sake.

— That's what they always asked. When I was tending.

— Here we are.

— No, really. Do you ever ask him to change a lightbulb or something?

Leslie was searching for the key to her door.

— That's the super, Leslie said. He's another story.

As they went in, she said,

— I don't think there's anything here but scotch. That's OK, isn't it? Bunning drank up everything else.

She went to the kitchen to get glasses and ice. Kathrin sat on the couch with Jane.

— Are you still seeing Andrew? she said.

— Off and on, Jane said.

— Off and on, that's what I'm looking for. On and off is more like it.

Leslie came back with the glasses and ice. She began to make drinks.

— Well, here's to you, she said. Here's to me. It's going to be hard moving out of here.

— You're not going to get to keep the apartment? Kathrin said.

— Twenty-six hundred a month? I couldn't afford it.

— Aren't you going to get something from Bunning?

— I'm not going to ask for anything. Some of the furniture—I can probably use that—and maybe a little something to get me by the first three or four months. I can stay with my mother if I have to. I hope I don't have to. Or I could stay with you, couldn't I? she asked Kathrin.

Kathrin had a walk-up on Lexington, one room painted black with mirrors on one wall.

— Of course. Until one of us killed the other, Kathrin said.

— If I had a boyfriend, it would be no problem, Leslie said, but I was too busy taking care of Bunning to have a boyfriend.

— You're lucky, she said to Jane, you've got Andy.

— Not really.

— What happened?

— Nothing, really. He wasn't serious.

— About you.

— That was part of it.

— So, what happened? Leslie said.

— I don't know. I just wasn't interested in the things he was interested in.

— Such as? Kathrin said.

— Everything.

— Give us an idea.

— The usual stuff.

— What?

— Anal sex, Jane said. She'd made it up, on an impulse. She wanted to break through somehow.

— Oh, God, Kathrin said. Makes me think of my ex.

— Malcolm, said Leslie, so, where is Malcolm? Are you still in touch?

— He's over in Europe. No, I never hear from him.

Malcolm wrote for a business magazine. He was short, but a very careful dresser—beautiful, striped suits and shined shoes.

— I wonder how I ever married him, Kathrin said. I wasn't very foresighted.

— Oh, I can see how it happened, Leslie said. In fact, I *saw* how it happened. He's very sexy.

— For one thing, it was because of his sister. She was great. We were friends from the first minute. God, this is strong, Kathrin said.

— You want a little more water?

— Yes. She gave me my first oyster. Am I supposed to *eat* that? I said. I'll show you how, she said, just throw them back and swallow. It was at the bar in Grand Central. Once I had them I couldn't stop. She was so completely up front. Are you sleeping with Malcolm? she asked me. We'd hardly met. She wanted to know what it was like, if he was as good as he looked.

Kathrin had drunk a lot of wine in the restaurant and a cocktail before that. Her lips glistened.

— What was her name? Jane asked.

— Enid.

— Oh, beautiful name.

— So, anyway, he and I went off—this was before we were married. We had this room with nothing in it but a window and a bed. That's when I was introduced to it.

— To what? Leslie said.

— In the ass.

— And?

— I liked it.

Jane was suddenly filled with admiration for her, admiration and embarrassment. This was not like the thing she had made up, it was actual. Why couldn't I ever admit something like that? she thought.

— But you got divorced, she said.

— Well, there's a lot beside that in life. We got divorced because I got tired of him chasing around. He was always covering stories in one place or another, but one time in London the phone rang at two in the morning and he went into the next room to talk. That's when I found out. Of course, she was just one of them.

— You're not drinking, Leslie said to Jane.

— Yes, I am.

— Anyway, we got divorced, Kathrin went on. So, now it'll be both of us, she said to Leslie. Join the club.

— Are you really getting divorced? Jane asked.

— It'll be a relief.

— How long has it been? Six years?

— Seven.

— That's a long time.

— A very long time.

— How did you meet? Jane said.

— How did we meet? Through bad luck, Leslie said—she was pouring more scotch into her glass. Actually, we met when he fell off a boat. I was going out with his cousin at the time. We were sailing, and Bunning claimed he had to do it to get my attention.

— That's so funny.

— Later, he changed his story and said he fell and it had to be *some*where.

Bunning's first name was actually Arthur, Arthur Bunning Hasset, but he hated the Arthur. Everyone liked him. His family owned a button factory and a big house in Bedford called Ha Ha, where he was brought up. In theory he wrote plays, at least one of which was close to being a success and had an off-Broadway run, but after that things became difficult. He had a secretary named Robin—she was called his assistant—who found him incredible and unpredictable, not to mention hilarious, and Leslie herself had always been amused by him, at least for several years, but then the drinking started.

The end had come a week or so before. They were invited to an opening night by a theatrical lawyer and his wife. First there was dinner, and at the restaurant, Bunning, who had started drinking at the apartment, ordered a martini.

— Don't, Leslie said.

He ignored her and was entertaining for a while but then sat silent and drinking while Leslie and the couple went on with the conversation. Suddenly Bunning said in a clear voice,

— Who are these people?

There was a silence.

— Really, who are they? Bunning asked again.

The lawyer coughed a little.

— We're their guests, Leslie said coldly.

Bunning's thoughts seemed to pass to something else and a few moments later he got up to go to the men's room. Half an hour passed. Finally Leslie saw him at the bar. He was drinking another martini. His expression was unfocused and childlike.

— Where've you been? he asked. I've been looking all over for you.

She was infuriated.

— This is the end, she said.

— No, really, where have you been? he insisted.

She began to cry.

— I'm going home, he decided.

Still, she remembered the summer mornings in New England when they were first married. Outside the window the squirrels were running down the trunk of a great tree, headfirst, curling to the unseen side of it, their wonderful bushy tails. She remembered driving to little summer theaters, the old iron bridges, cows lying in the wide doorway of a barn, cut cornfields, the smooth slow look of nameless rivers, the beautiful, calm countryside—how happy one is.

— You know, she said, Marge is crazy about him. Marge was her mother. That should have been the tip-off.

She went to get more ice and in the hallway caught sight of herself in a mirror.

— Have you ever decided this is as far as you can go? she said, coming back in.

— What do you mean? said Kathrin.

Leslie sat down beside her. They were really two of a kind, she decided. They'd been bridesmaids at one another's wedding. They were truly close.

— I mean, have you ever looked at yourself in the mirror and said, I can't . . . this is it.

— What do you mean?

— With men.

— You're just sore at Bunning.

— Who really needs them?

— Are you kidding?

— You want me to tell you something I've found out?

— What?

— I don't know . . . Leslie said helplessly.

— What were you going to say?

— Oh. My theory . . . My theory is, they remember you longer if you don't do it.

— Maybe, Kathrin said, but then, what's the point?

— It's just my theory. They want to divide and conquer.

— Divide?

— Something like that.

Jane had had less to drink. She wasn't feeling well. She had spent the afternoon waiting to talk to the doctor and emerging onto the unreal street.

She was wandering around the room and picked up a photograph of Leslie and Bunning taken around the time they got married.

— So, what's going to happen to Bunning? she asked.

— Who knows? Leslie said. He's going to go on like he's going. Some woman will decide she can straighten him out. Let's dance. I feel like dancing.

She made for the CD player and began looking through the CDs until she found one she liked and put it on. There was a moment's pause and then an uneven, shrieking wail began, much too loud. It was bagpipes.

— Oh, God, she cried, stopping it. It was in the wrong . . . it's one of his.

She found another and a low, insistent drumbeat started slowly, filling the room. She began dancing to it. Kathrin began, too. Then a singer or several of them became part of it, repeating the same words over and over. Kathrin paused to take a drink.

— Don't, Leslie said. Don't drink too much.

— Why?

— You won't be able to perform.

— Perform what?

Leslie turned to Jane and motioned.

— Come on.

— No, I don't really . . .

— Come on.

The three of them were dancing to the hypnotic, rhythmic singing. It went on and on. Finally Jane sat down, her face moist, and watched. Women often danced together or even alone, at parties. Did Bunning dance? she wondered. No, he wasn't the sort, nor was he embarrassed by it. He drank too much to dance, but really why did he drink? He didn't seem to care about things, but he probably cared very much, beneath.

Leslie sat down beside her.

— I hate to think about moving, she said, her head lolled back carelessly. I'm going to have to find some other place. That's the worst part.

She raised her head.

— In two years, Bunning's not even going to remember me. Maybe he'll say "my ex-wife" sometimes. I wanted to have a baby. He didn't like the idea. I said to him, I'm ovulating, and he said, that's wonderful. Well, that's how it is. I'll have one next time. If there is a next time. You have beautiful breasts, she said to Jane.

Jane was struck silent. She would never have had the courage to say something like that.

— Mine are saggy already, Leslie said.

— That's all right, Jane replied foolishly.

— I suppose I could have something done if I had the money. You can fix anything if you have the money.

It was not true, but Jane said,

— I guess you're right.

She had more than sixty thousand dollars she had saved or made from an oil company one of her colleagues had told her about. If she wanted to, she could buy a car, a Porsche Boxster came to mind. She wouldn't even have to sell the oil stock, she could get a loan and pay it off over three or four years and on weekends drive out to the country, to Connecticut, the little coastal towns, Madison, Old Lyme, Niantic, stopping somewhere to have lunch in a place that, in her imagination, was painted white outside. Perhaps there would be a man there, by himself, or even with some other men. He wouldn't have to fall off a boat. It wouldn't be Bunning, of course, but someone like him, wry, a little shy, the man she had somehow failed to meet until then. They'd have dinner, talk. They'd go to Venice, a thing she'd always wanted to do, in the winter, when no one else was there. They'd have a room above the canal and his shirts and shoes, a half-full bottle of she didn't bother to think of exactly what, some Italian wine, and perhaps some books. The sea air from the Adriatic would come in the window at night and she would wake early, before it was really light, to see him sleeping beside her, sleeping and breathing softly.

Beautiful breasts. That was like saying, I love you. She was warmed by it. She wanted to tell Leslie something but it wasn't the time, or maybe it was. She hadn't quite told herself yet.

Another number began and they were dancing again, coming together occasionally, arms flowing, exchanging smiles. Kathrin was like someone at one of the clubs, glamorous, uncaring. She had passion, daring. If you said something, she wouldn't even hear you. She was a kind of cheap goddess and would go on like that for a long time, spending too much for something that caught her fancy, a silk dress or pants, black and clinging, that widened at the bottom, the kind Jane would have with her in Venice. She hadn't had a love affair in college—she was the only one she knew who hadn't. Now she was sorry, she wished she'd had. And gone to the room with only a window and a bed.

— I have to go, she said.

— What? Leslie said over the music.

— I have to go.

— This has been fun, Leslie said, coming over to her.

They embraced in the doorway, awkwardly, Leslie almost falling down.

— Talk to you in the morning, she said.

Outside, Jane caught a cab, a clean one as it happened, and gave the driver her address near Cornelia Street. They started off, moving fast through the traffic. In the rearview mirror the driver, who was young, saw that Jane, a nice-looking girl about his age, was crying. At a red light next to a drugstore where it was well lit, he could see the tears streaming down her face.

— Excuse me, is something wrong? he asked.

She shook her head. It seemed she nearly answered.

— What is it? he said.

— Nothing, she said, shaking her head. I'm dying.

— You're sick?

— No, not sick. I'm dying of cancer, she said.

She had said it for the first time, listening to herself. There were four levels and she had the fourth, Stage Four.

— Ah, he said, are you sure?

The city was filled with so many strange people he could not tell if she was telling the truth or just imagining something.

— You want to go to the hospital? he asked.

— No, she said, unable to stop crying. I'm all right, she told him.

Her face was appealing though streaked with tears. He raised his head a little to see the rest of her. Appealing, too. But what if she is speaking the truth? he wondered. What if God, for whatever reason, has decided to end the life of someone like this? You cannot know. That much he understood.

Give

————◆————

IN THE MORNING—it was my wife's birthday, her thirty-first—we slept a little late, and I was at the window looking down at Des in a bathrobe with his pale hair awry and a bamboo stick in his hand. He was deflecting and sometimes with a flourish making a lunge. Billy, who was six then, was hopping around in front of him. I could hear his shrieks of joy. Anna came up beside me.

— What are they doing now?

— I can't tell. Billy is waving something over his head.

— I think it's a flyswatter, she said, disbelieving.

She was just thirty-one, the age when women are past foolishness though not unfeeling.

— Look at him, she said. Don't you just love him?

The grass was brown from summer and they were dancing around on it. Des was barefoot, I noticed. It was early for him to be up. He often slept until noon and then managed to slip gracefully into the rhythm of the household. That was his talent, to live as he liked, almost without concern, to live as if he would reach the desired end one way or another and not be bothered by whatever came between. It included being com-

60

mitted several times, once for wandering out on Moore Street naked. None of the psychiatrists had any idea who he was. None of them had ever read a damned thing, he said. Some of the patients had.

He was a poet, of course. He even *looked* like a poet, intelligent, lank. He'd won the Yale prize when he was twenty-five and went on from there. When you pictured him, it was wearing a gray herringbone jacket, khaki pants, and for some reason sandals. Doesn't fit together, but a lot of things about him were like that. Born in Galveston, ROTC in college, and even married while an undergraduate, although what became of that wife he never clearly explained. His real life came after that, and he had lived it ever since, teaching sometimes in community classes, traveling to Greece and Morocco, living there for a period, having a breakdown, and through it all writing the poem that had made his name. I read the poem, a third of it anyway, standing stunned in a bookshop in the Village. I remember the afternoon, cloudy and quiet, and I remember, too, almost leaving myself, the person I was, the ordinary way I felt about things, my perception of—there's no other word for it—the depth of life, and above all the thrill of successive lines. The poem was an aria, jagged and unending. Its tone was what set it apart—written as if from the shades. *There lay the delta, there the burning arms* . . . was the way it began, and immediately I felt it was not about rivers uncoiling but about desire. It revealed itself only slowly, like some kind of dream, *the light fluttering on the fronds*, with names and nouns, Naples, worn benches, Luxor and the kings, Salonika, small waves falling on the stones. There was repetition, even refrain. Lines that seemed unconnected gradually became part of a confession that had at its center rooms in the burning heat of August where something has taken place, clearly sexual, but it is also the vacant streets of rural Texas, roads, forgotten friends, the slap of hands on rifle slings and forked pennants limp at parades. There are condoms, sun-faded cars, soiled menus with misspellings, a kind of pyre on which he had laid his life. That was why he seemed so pure—he had given all. Everyone lies about their lives, but he had not lied about his. He had made of it a noble lament, through it always running this thing you have had, that you will always have, but can never have. *There stood Erechtheus, polished limbs and greaves . . . come to me, Hellas, I long for your touch.*

I had met him at a party and only managed to say, — I read your beautiful poem. He was unexpectedly open in a way that impressed me and straightforward in a way that was unflinching. In talking, he mentioned the title of a book or two and referred to some things he assumed I would, of course, know, and he was witty, all of that but something more; his language invited me to be joyous, to speak as the gods—I use the plural because it's hard to think of him as obedient to a single god—had intended. We were always speaking of things that it turned out, oddly enough, both of us knew about although he knew more. Lafcadio Hearn, yes, of course he knew who that was and even the name of the Japanese widow he married and the town they lived in, though he had never been to Japan himself. Arletty, Nestor Almendros, Jacques Brel, The Lawrenceville Stories, the *cordon sanitaire*, everything including his real interest, jazz, to which I only weakly responded. The Answer Man, Billy Cannon, the Hellespont, Stendhal on love, it was as if we had sat in the same classes and gone to the same cities. And there was Billy, swatting at his legs.

Billy loved him, he was almost a pal. He had an infectious laugh and was always ready to play. During the times he stayed with us, he made ships out of sofa cushions and swords and shields from whatever was in the garage. When he owned his car, the engine of which would cut out every so often, he claimed that turning the radio on and off would fix it, the circuits had been miswired or something. Billy was in charge of the radio.

— Oh, oh, Des would say, there it goes. Radio!

And Billy, with huge pleasure, would turn the radio on and off, on and off. How to explain why this worked? It was the power of a poet or maybe even a trick.

On Anna's birthday, at about noon a beautiful arrangement of flowers, lilies and yellow roses, was delivered. They were from him. That evening we had dinner with some friends at the Red Bar, always noisy but the table was in the small room past the bar. I hadn't ordered a birthday cake because we were going to have one back at the house, a rum cake, her favorite. Billy sat in her lap as she put her rings, one after another, carefully over separate candles, each ring for a wish.

— Will you help me blow them out? she said to Billy, her face close to his hair.

— Too many, he said.

— Oh, God, you really know how to hurt a woman.

— Go ahead, Des told him. If you don't have enough breath, I'll catch it and send it back.

— How do you do that?

63

— I can do it. Haven't you heard of someone catching their breath?

— They're burning down, Anna said. Come on, one, two, three!

The two of them blew them out. Billy wanted to know what her wishes had been, but she wouldn't tell.

We ate the cake, just the four of us, and I gave her the present I knew she would love. It was a wristwatch, very thin and square with Roman numerals and a small blue stone, I think tourmaline, embedded in the stem. There are not many things more beautiful than a watch lying new in its case.

— Oh, Jack! she said. It's gorgeous!

She showed it to Billy and then to Des.

— Where did you get it? Then, looking, Cartier, she said.

— Yes.

— I *love* it.

Beatrice Hage, a woman we knew, had one like it that she had inherited from her mother. It had an elegance that defied the years and demands of fashion.

It was easy to find things she would like. Our taste was the same, it had been from the first. It would be impossible to live with someone otherwise. I've always thought it was the most important single thing, though people may not realize it. Perhaps it's transmitted to them in the way someone dresses or, for that matter, undresses, but taste is a thing no one is born with, it's learned, and at a certain point it can't be altered. We sometimes talked about that, what could and couldn't be altered. People were always saying something had completely changed them, some experience or book or man, but if you knew how they had been before, nothing much really had changed. When you found someone who was tremendously appealing but not quite perfect, you might believe you could change them after marriage, not everything, just a few things, but in truth the most you could expect was to change perhaps one thing and even that would eventually go back to what it had been.

The small things that could be overlooked at first but in time became annoying, we had a way of handling, of getting the pebble out of the shoe, so to speak. It was called a give, and it was agreed that it would last. The phrase that was overused, an eating habit, even a piece of favorite clothing, a give was a request to abandon it. You couldn't ask *for* something, only to stop something. The wide skirt of the bathroom sink was always wiped dry because of a give. Anna's little finger no longer extended when she drank from a cup. There might be more than one thing you would like to ask, and there was sometimes difficulty in choosing, but there was the satisfaction of knowing that once a year, without causing resentment, you would be able to ask your husband or wife to stop this one thing.

Des was downstairs when we put Billy to bed. I was in the hall when Anna came out holding her finger to her lips and having turned off the light.

— Is he asleep?

— Yes.

— Well, happy birthday, I said.

— Yes.

There was something odd in the way she said it. She stood there, her long neck and blond hair.

— What is it, darling?

She said nothing for a moment. Then she said,

— I want a give.

— All right, I said.

I don't know why, I felt nervous.

— What would you like?

— I want you to stop it with Des, she said.

— Stop it? Stop what?

My heart was skipping.

— Stop the sex, she said.

I knew she was going to say it. I had hoped something else, and the words were like a thick curtain tumbling down or a plate smashing on the floor.

— I don't know what you're talking about.

Her face was hard,

— Yes, you do. You know exactly what I'm talking about.

— Darling, you're mistaken. There's nothing going on with Des. He's a friend, he's my closest friend.

The tears began to run down her face.

— Don't, I said. Please. Don't cry. You're wrong.

— I have to cry, she said, her voice unsteady. Anyone would cry. You have to do it. You have to stop. We promised one another.

— Oh, God, you're imagining this.

— Please, she begged, don't. Please, please, don't.

She was wiping her cheeks as if to make herself again presentable.

— You have to do what we promised, she said. You have to give.

There are things you cannot give, that would simply crush your heart. It was half of life she was asking for, him slipping off his watch, holding him, having him in your possession, in

66

indescribable happiness, in love with you. Nothing else could be like that. There was an apartment on 12th Street that we were able to use, the garden behind it, the dazzling chords of *Petroushka*—the record happened to be there and we used to play it—chords that would always, as long as I lived, bring me back to it, his pliancy and slow smile.

— I'm not doing anything with Des, I said. I swear to you.

— You swear to me.

— Yes.

— And I'm supposed to believe you.

— I swear to you.

She looked away.

— All right, she said at last.

A great joy filled me. Then she said,

— All right. But he has to leave. For good. If you want me to believe you, that's what it takes.

— Anna . . .

— No, that's the proof.

— How can I tell him to leave? What's the reason?

— Make up something. I don't care.

IN THE MORNING he got up late and was in the kitchen, the smoothness of sleep still on him. Anna had gone off. My hands were trembling.

— Good morning, he said with a smile.

— Good morning.

I couldn't bring myself to it. All I could say was,

— Des . . .

— Yes?

— I don't know what to say.

— About what?

— Us. It's over.

He seemed not to understand.

— What's over?

— Everything. I feel like I'm coming apart inside.

— Ah, he said in a soft way. I see. Maybe I see. What happened?

— It's just that you can't stay.

— Anna, he guessed.

— Yes.

— She knows.

— Yes. I don't know what to do.

— Could I talk to her, do you think?

— It wouldn't do any good. Believe me.

— But we've always gotten along. What difference does it make? Let me talk to her.

— She doesn't want to, I lied.

— When did all this happen?

— Last night. Don't ask me how it came about. I don't know.

He sighed. He said something I didn't get. All I could hear was my own heart beating. He left later that day.

I felt the injustice for a long time. He'd brought only pleasure to us, and if to me particularly, that didn't diminish it. I had some photographs that I kept in a certain place, and of course I had the poems. I followed him from afar, the way a woman does a man she was never able to marry. The glittering blue water slid past as he made his way between the islands. There was Ios, white in the haze, where the dust of Homer lay, they said.

Platinum

The Brule apartment had a magnificent view of the park, bare and vast in winter and in the summer a rich sea of green. The apartment was in a fine building, narrow but tall, and it was in a way comforting to think of how many others there were, dignified and calm, building upon fine building, all with their unsmiling doormen and solemn entrances. Rare carpets, servants, expensive furniture. Brule had paid more than nine hundred thousand for it at a time when prices were high, but the apartment was worth far more now, priceless, in fact. It had high ceilings, afternoon sunlight, and wide doors with curved brass handles. There were deep armchairs, flowers, tables dense with photographs, and many pictures on the walls, including Vollard prints in the hallway that led to the bedrooms and a ravishing dark painting by Camille Bombois.

Brule was one of those men about whom more is rumored than known. He was in his fifties and successful. He had defended some notorious clients and, less publicized, was said to have done unpaid work for those with no resources

or hope. Details were vague. He had a soft voice that nevertheless carried authority and iron beneath a calm smile. He
walked to work, perhaps a mile down the avenue, in a cash-
mere overcoat and scarf during the winter, and the doormen,
who murmured good morning, received five hundred dollars apiece at Christmas. He was a figure of decency and
honor, and like the old men described by Cicero who planted
orchards they would not live to see the fruit from, but who
did it out of a sense of responsibility and respect for the gods,
he had a desire to bequeath the best of what he had known to
his descendants.

His wife, Pascale, who was French, was warm and understanding. She was his second wife and had herself been married before, to a famous Parisian jeweler. She had no children
of her own and her only fault, Brule felt, was she didn't like to
cook. She couldn't cook and talk at the same time, she said.
She was not beautiful but had an intelligent, faintly Asiatic
face. Her generosity and good instincts were inborn.

— Look, she had said to his daughters when she and Brule
were married, I'm not your mother and I can never be, but I
hope that we'll be friends. If we are, good, and if not, you can
still count on me for anything.

The daughters were young girls at the time. As it turned
out, they loved her. The three of them and their husbands and
children came on all the holidays and often, though not all
at once, of course, for dinner. They were an intimate and
devoted family, a matter of great pride to Brule, the more so
since his first marriage had failed.

You belonged to the family, not as someone who happened
to be married to a daughter, but entirely. You were one of

them, one for all and all for one. The oldest daughter, Grace, had told her husband,

— You have to really get used to the plural of things now.

Brian Woodra had married Sally, the youngest, on a glorious summer day on a lawn set with countless white chairs, the women in clinging dresses. Sally was in a gown of white, stiffened silk, sleeveless, with wide shoulder straps and her dark hair gleaming on her slender back. Her ears had fluted, silvery earrings and her face was filled with joy and the occasional concern that things go right, a lovely face with only the barest hint of smallness behind it and you instantly saw the expense of her upbringing. A New York girl, smart and assured. She'd gone to Skidmore, where she roomed with two nymphomaniacs, she liked to say, wanting to shock.

The groom was no taller than she was and slightly bow-legged with a wide jaw and winning smile. He was lively and well liked. His friends from college and even prep school came to the wedding and rose to give their fond recollections of him and predict the worst. At the moment of vows he found himself overcome by his wife-to-be's purity and beauty, as if it were for the first time fully revealed.

The great tent in which the wedding dinner was held had long tables with large arrangements of flowers. As evening came, the tent slowly bloomed with light from within like an immense, ethereal ship, destined for voyage on the sea or in the heavens, one could not tell. Brule told his new son-in-law that he, Brian, was now to know the greatest happiness that one could experience on earth, referring to matrimony, of course.

For a wedding present they were given a cruise in the wake

of Odysseus along the Anatolian coast, and in not much more than a year their first child came, a little girl they named Lily, loving and good-natured. Sally was a mother who, though completely involved in her child, still found time for all the rest, entertaining, seeing films, dinners with her husband, equality, friends. The apartment was a little on the dark side, but she did not expect to be in it forever. Grace lived just ten blocks away with her husband and two children, and Eva, the middle sister, was married to a sculptor and lived downtown.

Lily was delicious. From the beginning she loved to be in bed with her mother and father, especially her father, and when she was three whispered to him in adoration,

— I want to be yours.

Two years later, as a reward, to make up for all the attention given to her new little brother, Brian took her to Paris for five days, just the two of them. In retrospect it was the moment of her childhood he cherished most. She behaved like a woman, a companion. It was impossible to love her more. They ate breakfast in the room and wrote postcards together, took the long, arrowy boat up and down the Seine, beneath the bridges, went to the bird market and the museums, Versailles, and in the giant Ferris wheel near the Concorde one afternoon rose high above the city, alarmingly high; Brian himself was frightened.

— Do you like it? he asked.

— I'm trying to, she said.

No one is braver than you, he thought.

At day's end—the light was just fading—he felt spent. At the hotel, near the reception, there was a Canadian couple waiting for a taxi. Lily was watching the indicator light for the elevator, which had remained for a long time at the fifth floor.

— Is it broken, Daddy?

— It's just someone taking their time.

He could hear the couple talking. The woman, blond and smooth-browed, was in a glittering silver top. They were going out for the evening, into the stream of lights, boulevards, restaurants brimming with talk. He had only a glimpse of them setting forth, the light on her hair, the cab door held open for her, and for a moment forgot that he had everything.

— Here it comes, he heard his daughter call, Daddy, here it comes.

In late April was Michael Brule's fifty-eighth birthday. For gifts he had asked only for things to eat or drink, but Del, Eva's husband, had carved a beautiful wooden seabird for him, unpainted and on legs thin as straws. Brule was deeply touched.

Brian was in the kitchen cooking. It was noisy. The children were playing some kind of game, to the annoyance of the dog, an old Scottie.

— Don't frighten her! Don't frighten her! they cried.

It was risotto Brian was making, adding warm broth in small amounts and stirring slowly, to the rapt attention of one of the girls hired to help serve.

— It's almost ready, he called. He could hear the family voices, the dog barking, the laughter.

The girl, in a white shirt and velvety pants, was watching in fascination. He held out the wooden spoon on which there was a sample.

— Want to taste it? he asked.

— Yes, darling, she said.

Ssh, he gestured playfully. Not looking at him, she took the portion of rice between her lips. Pamela was her name.

She wasn't really a caterer; she worked at the U.N. She and the other girl were hired by the hour.

Her legs Brian saw when she came into the bar at the U.N. Hotel and sat down beside him with a smile, completely at ease. He had been nervous, but it left him immediately. From the first moment he felt a thrilling, natural complicity. His heart filled with excitement, like a sail.

— So, he began, Pamela . . .

— Pam.

— Would you like a drink?

— Is that white wine?

— Yes.

— Good. White wine.

She was twenty-two, from Pennsylvania, but with some kind of rare, natural polish.

— I must say, you are . . . he said, then felt suddenly cautious.

— What?

— Definitely good-looking.

— Oh, I don't know.

— It's unarguable. I'm just curious, he said, how much do you weigh?

— A hundred and sixteen.

— That's what I would have thought.

— Really?

— No, but anything you would have said.

She had told them she had a doctor's appointment and needed extra time for lunch. She told him that. As she entered the hotel elevator he could not help but notice her fine hips. Then, incredibly, they were in the room. His heart was uncontrollable and everything was prepared for them, the sleek furnishings, the chairs, the thick fresh towels in the bath. There had been four murders in Brooklyn the night before. The brokers were going wild on Wall Street. On Fourteenth, men stood in the cold beside tables of watches and socks. The madman on Fifty-seventh was singing arias at the top of his voice, buildings were being torn down, new towers rising. She rose to draw the drapes and for a moment stood in the space between them, in the light and looking down. The splendor and newness of her! He had known nothing like it.

Her apartment was borrowed, from someone on assignment. Even at that, it was sparsely furnished. He wanted to give her something every time he saw her, a gift, something unexpected, a chrome and leather chair that he showed her in the window before he ordered it delivered, a ring, a rosewood box, but he was careful to keep nothing that came from her—note, e-mail, photograph—that might betray him. There was one exception, a picture he had taken as she half sat up in bed, from over her bare shoulder, breasts, smooth stomach, thighs, you would not know who it was. He kept it at work between the pages of a book. He liked to turn to it and remember.

In those days of desire so deep that it left him empty-legged, he did not behave unnaturally at home—if anything he was more loving and devoted although Lily, especially, was beyond increased devotion. He came home filled with forbidden happiness, forbidden but unrivalled, and embraced his wife and played with or read to his children. The prohibited feeds the appetite for all the rest. He went from one to the other with a heart that was pure. On Park Avenue he stood on the island in the middle, waiting to cross. The traffic lights were turning red as far as he could see. The distant buildings stood majestic in the monied haze. Beside him were people in coats and hats, with packages, briefcases, none of them as fortunate as he. The city was a paradise. The glory of it was that it sheltered his singular life.

— Am I your mistress? she asked one day.

— Mistress? No, he thought, that was something older, even old-fashioned. He knew of no word to truly describe her other than probable downfall or perhaps fate.

— What's your wife like? she said.

— My wife?

— You'd rather not talk about her.

— No, you'd like her.

— That would be just my luck.

— She doesn't have quite your ideas of how to live.

— I don't know how to live.

— Yes, you do.

— I don't think so.

— You have something not a lot of people have.

— What's that?

— Real nerve.

When he came home that evening, his wife said,

— Brian, there's something I want to talk to you about, something I have to ask you.

He felt his heart skip. His children were running toward him.

— Daddy!

— Daddy and I have to talk for a minute, Sally told them.

She led him into the living room.

— What's up? he said as calmly as he could.

Grace and Harry, it turned out, wanted to come with their children and share the gardener's cottage during the two weeks in August that Lily would be off at sleepaway camp and some arrangement could be made for Ian so that Sally and Brian could have some time to themselves. Now that would be impossible.

She went on talking, but Brian barely listened. He was still hearing her first words that had been so frightening. He was rehearsing replies to a far more serious question. He would tell her the truth, could he do that? The truth was essential, yet it was the thing least wanted.

— We should do this over a drink, he would say. We should do it when we're calmer.

— I'm not going to be calmer.

He had to somehow put it off until she was the way she often was, clever and understanding. He would say something about perspective.

— Just speak in plain English.

— You can't say it in plain English.

— Try, she said.

— You know these things happen. You're a smart woman. You know something about the world.

— Yes, tell me about it.

Her mouth was turned down, a corner of it trembling.

— There's been someone, but it's not important. Can't you see that it's not important?

— Get out of here, she said, and don't come back. Don't try to see the children, I won't let you. I'm going to change the locks.

— Sally, you can't do that. I could never live like that. Don't be melodramatic, please. That's not our kind of life. The words were beginning to jam up in his mouth. This is nothing unsolvable. You know very well that Pascale was your father's mistress, I won't guess for how long.

— They got married.

— That isn't the point.

He was beginning to stutter.

— What *is* the point?

— The point is there's a superior way of living we should be intelligent enough to understand.

— Which means you having some other woman?

— You're making this caustic. Don't, please. It's beneath us just to play roles. We're above that. You know that.

— All I know is that you're a cheat.

— I'm not a cheat.

— Daddy's going to kill you.

He couldn't find the words. Whatever he thought of was torn apart by her single-mindedness. But it would never come to this.

On the other hand, Pamela had a life of her own; that was the only flaw. She went out at night, there were parties. Some Tunisians from the delegation were very nice.

— Is that right? he said.

She'd gone to a party at the Four Seasons, she told him, and walked to work the next morning with a thousand dollars in her shoe, although she didn't say that. One of the Tunisians was particularly nice.

— They like to have fun, she said.

— You're turning into a playgirl, Brian said, a little sourly. How do I know you're not playing around with this guy?

— You'd know it.

— Maybe I would. Would you tell me? The truth? What's his name?

— Tahar.

— I wish you wouldn't.

— I'm not, she said.

In June, Sally and the children went to the country for the summer. For most of the week, Brian was in the city by himself.

— How was I lucky enough to meet you? he said.

They were having dinner amid the liveliness of the crowd, the intimacy within it, the voices all around. He had seen most of them. She was by far the prize of the room.

— We're going to be friends for a long time, she promised.

Summer mornings with their first, soft light. Amorous mornings, the red numbers flicking silently on the clock, the first sunlight in the trees. Her stunning naked back. The most sacred hours, he realized, of his life.

Dressing one morning, she asked,

— Whose are these?

In a folded packet on the night table had been a pair of shining earrings.

— Are they your wife's?

She was trying one on, fastening it to her ear. She turned her head one way and the other, looking at herself in the mirror.

— What are they, silver?

— They're platinum. Better than silver.

— They're your wife's.

— They were being repaired. I had to pick them up.

It was hard not to admire her, her bare neck, her aplomb.

— Can I borrow them? she asked.

— I can't. She knows I was supposed to pick them up.

— Just say they weren't ready.

— Darling . . .

— I'll give them back. Is that what you're afraid of? I'd just like to wear them once, something that's hers but at the moment mine.

— That's very Bette Davis.

— Who?

— Just be careful and don't lose them, he managed to say.

That was a Tuesday. Two nights later a terrible event occurred. It was at a reception given by a group dedicated to the Impressionists; Pascale was a supporter but was away that evening and couldn't attend. Sally had insisted that Brian go, and in the crowd coming up the stairway he had seen, with a stab of jealousy, more fierce because it was a complete surprise, Pamela. He began to push his way forward to see who she might be with.

— Hey, where are you going in such a hurry?

It was Del, his brother-in-law.

— Where have you been hiding?

— Hiding?

— We haven't seen you for weeks.

Brian liked him, but not at this moment.

— Why don't you come to dinner with us tonight, afterward?

— I can't, Brian said unthinkingly.

— Come on, we're going to Elio's, Del insisted. Look at all these women. Where do they come from? They weren't around when I was single.

Brian hardly heard him. Past his brother-in-law, near the windows not fifteen feet away, he could see Pamela talking to Michael Brule, not just exchanging a greeting but in some sort of conversation. She was wearing a pale blue dress, one he liked, cut low in back. Her dark hair was tied and he could see quite clearly, she was wearing the earrings. They were unmistakable. He moved a bit so as not to be observed, his heart beating furiously. Finally Brule was gone.

— Darling, you must be crazy, he said in a furious, low voice when he reached her.

— Hello, she said cheerfully.

There was always such life in that voice.

— What are you doing? he insisted.

— What do you mean?

— The earrings!

— I'm wearing them, she said.

— You can't wear them. That was my father-in-law. He bought them! He gave them to Sally! Why did you wear them here?

His voice was still low but people close by could hear the anxiety.

— How was I to know? Pamela said.

— Jesus, I knew I shouldn't have lent them to you.

— Oh, take the damned earrings, she said, suddenly annoyed.

— Don't do that.

She was taking them off. It was the first time he had seen her angry and suddenly he was frightened, afraid to be in her disfavor.

— Don't, please. I'm the one who should be angry, he said.

She pushed them into his hand.

— And yes, she said, he saw them. Then, with astounding confidence, Don't worry, he won't say anything.

— What do you mean? What makes you so sure? The answer suddenly struck him like an illness.

— Don't worry, he won't, she said.

Somebody was handing her a glass of wine.

— Thank you, she said calmly. This is Brian, a friend of mine. Brian, this is Tahar.

She did not answer the phone that night. The next day, his father-in-law called and asked to meet for lunch, it was important.

They met at a restaurant Brule favored, with formal service and a European-looking clientele. It was near his office. Brule was reading the menu when Brian arrived. He looked up. His glasses, which were rimless, caught the light in a way that made his eyes almost invisible.

— I'm glad you were able to come, he said, returning to the menu.

Brian made an effort to read the menu himself. He made some remark about not having had a chance to say hello the night before.

— I was extremely disturbed by what I learned last night, Brule said, as if not having heard.

The waiter stood reciting some dishes that were not on the menu. Brian was preparing his reply, but after they had ordered, it was Brule who continued.

— Your behavior isn't worthy of the husband of my daughter, he said.

— I don't know if you're in a position to say that, Brian managed.

— Please don't interrupt me. Let me finish. You'll have your chance afterward. I discover that you've been having an affair with a young woman—I'm aware of the details, believe me—and if you place any value at all on your wife and family, I would say you have put that in grave jeopardy. If Sally were to learn of it, I'm certain she would leave you and, under the circumstances, probably retain custody, and I would support her in that. Fortunately, she doesn't know, so there is still the possibility of this not being disastrous, providing you do the necessary thing.

There was a pause. It was as if Brian had been asked a bewildering question, the answer to which he should know. His thoughts were fluttering, however, ungraspable.

— What thing is that? he said, though knowing.

— You give up this girl and never see her again.

This wonderful girl, this smooth-shouldered girl.

— And what about you? Brian said as evenly as he could.

Brule ignored it.

— Otherwise, Brule continued, I'm loath to think of it, Sally will have to know.

Brian's jaw, despite his effort, was trembling. It was not only humiliation, there was a burning jealousy. His father-in-law seemed to hold every advantage. The manicured hands had touched her, the aging body had been imposed on hers. Some plates were served but Brian did not pick up his fork.

— She wouldn't be the only one to know, would she? Pascale would know everything, too, he said.

— If you mean you would try to implicate me, I can only say that would be futile and foolish.

— But you wouldn't be able to deny it, Brian said stubbornly.

— I'd most certainly deny it. It would just be seen as a frantic attempt to deflect your guilt and blacken others. No one would believe it, I assure you. Most important, Pamela would back me up.

— What an incredible, what a pompous statement. No, she won't.

— Yes, she will. I've taken care of that.

He was not to see or speak to her again, without explanation or any farewell.

— I don't believe it, Brian said.

He did not stay. He pushed back his chair, dropped his napkin on the table, and, excusing himself, left. Brule continued with lunch. He told the waiter to cancel the other order.

The earrings were still in his pocket. He set them in front of him and tried to call. She was away from her desk, her voice said. Please leave a message. He hung up. He felt a terrifying urgency; every minute was unbearable. He thought of going to her office but it would be difficult to talk to her there. She was away from her desk, in someone else's office. Even that caused him unhappiness and envy. He thought of the hotel bar. In she had come in a short black skirt and high heels, on her white neck an opaque, blue necklace. With Brule it could not have been anything but sordid, some suggestion in that low voice, some clumsy act on a couch. What could it have been on her part except resignation, finally? He called again, and three or four more times during the afternoon, leaving the message to please call back, it was important.

At six, he somehow made his way home. It was one of those evenings like the beginning of a marvelous performance in which everyone somehow had a role. Lights had come on in the windows, the sidewalk restaurants were filling, children were running home late from playing in the park, the promise of fulfillment was everywhere. In the elevator a pretty woman he did not recognize was carrying a large bunch of flowers somewhere upstairs. She avoided looking at him.

He let himself into his apartment and immediately felt its emptiness. The furniture stood silently. The kitchen seemed cold, as if it had never known use. He walked around aimlessly and dropped into a chair. It was six-thirty. She would be home by now, he decided. She wasn't. He made a drink and sat with it, sipping and thinking or rather letting the same helpless thoughts eat deeper, unalterable, as evening slowly filled the room. He turned on some lights and called her again.

The anguish was unbearable. She had been annoyed, but surely that was only at the moment. It could not be that. She had been frightened by Brule somehow. She was not the sort of person to be easily frightened. He made another drink and continued to call. Sometime after ten—his heart leapt—she answered.

— Oh, God, he said, I've been calling you all day. Where have you been? I've been frantic to talk to you. I had to have lunch with Brule; it was disgusting. I walked out. Has he talked to you?

— Yes, she said.

— I was afraid so. What did he say?

— It's not that.

— Of course it's that. He made some threats. Look, I'm coming over.

85

— No, don't.

— Then you come here.

— I can't, she said.

— Of course you can. You can do anything you want. I feel so terrible. He wanted to prevent me from talking to you. Listen, darling. This may take a little time to work out. We'll have to lie a little low. You know I'm crazy about you. You know no one in the world has ever meant more to me. Whatever he said, nothing can affect that.

— I suppose.

He felt something then, a crack, a fissure. He had the sense of something impending and unbearable.

— It's not you suppose. You know it. Tell me something, tell me the truth. When did it happen between you and him? I just want to know. Before?

— I don't want to talk about it now, she said.

— Just tell me.

Suddenly something he hadn't thought of came to him. He suddenly understood why she was so hesitant.

— Tell me one thing, he said. Does he want to keep seeing you?

— No.

— Is that the truth? You're telling me the truth?

Sitting in a chair near her, legs sprawled like a lord, was Tahar with a bored look of patience.

— Yes, it's the truth, she said.

— I don't know what the solution is, but I know there is one, Brian assured her.

Tahar could hear only her end of the conversation and did not know who it was with, but he made a slight motion with his chin that said, finish with that. Pam nodded a little in agreement. Tahar did not drink but he offered a powerful intoxicant: darkened skin, white teeth, and a kind of strange perfume that clung even to his clothes. He offered rooms above the souk with a view of the city one could not even imagine, nights of an intense blueness, mornings when you had drifted far from the familiar world. Brian was some-one she would remember, perhaps someone she could always call.

Tahar made another gesture of slight annoyance. For him, it was only the beginning.

Palm Court

———◆———

LATE ONE AFTERNOON, near the close, his assistant,
Kenny, palm over the mouthpiece, said there was someone named Noreen on the phone.

— You know her, she says.

— Noreen? I'll take it, Arthur said. Just a minute.

He got up and closed the door to his cubicle. He was still
visible through the glass as he sat and turned toward the window, distancing himself from all that was going on, the doz-
ens of customers' men, some of them women, which once
would have been unthinkable, looking at their screens and
talking on the phone. His heart was tripping faster when he
spoke.

— Hello?

— Arthur?

The one word and a kind of shiver went through him, a
frightened happiness, as when your name is called by the
teacher.

— It's Noreen, she said.

— Noreen. How are you? God, it's been a long time. Where
are you?

— I'm here. I'm living back here now, she said.

— No kidding. What happened?

— We broke up.

— That's too bad, he said. I'm sorry to hear that.

He always seemed completely sincere, even in the most ordinary comments.

— It was a mistake, she said. I never should have done it. I should have known.

The floor around the desk was strewn with paper, reports, annual statements with their many numbers. That was not his strength. He liked to talk to people, he could talk and tell stories all day. And he was known to be honest. He had taken as models the old-timers, men long gone such as Henry Braver, Patsy Millinger's father, who'd been a partner and had started before the war. Onassis had been one of his clients. Braver had an international reputation as well as a nose for the real thing. Arthur didn't have the nose, but he could talk and listen. There were all kinds of ways of making money in this business. His way was finding one or two big winners to go down and double on. And he talked to his clients every day.

— Mark, how are you, tootsula? You ought to be here. The numbers came in on Micronics. They're all crying. We were so smart not to get involved in that. Sweetheart, you want to know something? There are some very smart guys here who've taken a bath. He lowered his voice. Morris, for one.

— Morris? They should give him an injection. Put him to sleep.

— He was a little too smart this time. Living through the Depression didn't help this time.

Morris had a desk near the copy machine, a courtesy desk.

He had been a partner, but after he retired there was nothing to do—he hated Florida and didn't play golf—and so he came back to the firm and traded for himself. His age alone set him apart. He was a relic with perfect, false teeth and lived in some amberoid world with an aged wife. They all joked about him. The years had left him, as if marooned, alone at his desk and in an apartment on Park Avenue no one had ever been to.

Morris had lost a lot on Micronics. It was impossible to say how much. He kept his own shaky figures, but Arthur had gotten it out of Marie, the sexless woman who cleared trades.

— A hundred thousand, she said. Don't say anything.

— Don't worry, darling, Arthur told her.

Arthur knew everything and was on the phone all day. It was one unending conversation: gossip, affection, news. He looked like Punch, with a curved nose, up-pointing chin, and innocent smile. He was filled with happiness, but the kind that knew its limits. He had been at Frackman, Wells from the time there were seven employees, and now there were nearly two hundred with three floors in the building. He himself had become rich, beyond anything he could have imagined, although his life had not changed and he still had the same apartment in London Terrace. He was living there the night he first met Noreen in Goldie's. She did something few girls had ever done with him, she laughed and sat close. From the first moment there was openness between them. Noreen. The piano rippling away, the old songs, the noise.

— I'm divorced, she said. How about you?

— Me? The same, he said.

The street below was filled with hurrying people, cars. The sound of it was faint.

— Really? she said.

It had been years since he had talked to her. There was a time they had been inseparable. They were at Goldie's every night or at Clarke's, where he also went regularly. They always gave him a good table, in the middle section with the side door or in back with the crowd and the unchanging menu written neatly in chalk. Sometimes they stood in front at the long, scarred bar with the sign that said under no circumstances would women be served there. The manager, the bartenders, waiters, everybody knew him. Clarke's was his real home; he merely went elsewhere to sleep. He drank very little despite his appearance, but he always paid for drinks and stayed at the bar for hours, occasionally taking a few steps to the men's room, a pavilion of its own, long and old-fashioned, where you urinated like a grand duke on blocks of ice. To Clarke's came advertising men, models, men like himself, and off-duty cops late at night. He showed Noreen how to recognize them, black shoes and white socks. Noreen loved it. She was a favorite there, with her looks and wonderful laugh. The waiters called her by her first name.

Noreen was dark blond, though her mother was Greek, she said. There were a lot of blonds in the north of Greece where her family came from. The ranks of the Roman legions had become filled with Germanic tribesmen as time passed, and when Rome fell some of the scattered legions settled in the mountains of Greece; at least that was the way she had heard it.

— So I'm Greek but I'm German, too, she told Arthur.

— God, I hope not, he said. I couldn't go with a German.

— What do you mean?

— Be seen with.

— Arthur, she explained, you have to accept the way things are, what I am and what you are and why it's so good.

There were things she wanted to tell him but didn't, things he wouldn't like to hear, or so she felt. About being a young girl and the night at the St. George Hotel when she was nineteen and went upstairs with a guy she thought was really nice. They went to his boss's suite. The boss was away and they were drinking his twelve-year-old scotch, and the next thing she knew she was lying facedown on the bed with her hands tied behind her. That was in a different world than Arthur's. His was decent, forgiving, warm.

They went together for nearly three years, the best years. They saw one another almost every night. She knew all about his work. He could make it seem so interesting, the avid individuals, the partners, Buddy Frackman, Warren Sender. And Morris; she had actually seen Morris once on the elevator.

— You're looking very well, she told him nervily.

— You, too, he said, smiling.

He didn't know who she was, but a few moments later he leaned toward her and silently formed the words,

— Eighty-seven.

— Really?

— Yes, he said proudly.

— I'd never guess.

She knew how, one day coming back from lunch, Arthur and Buddy had seen Morris lying in the street, his white shirt covered with blood. He had accidentally fallen, and there were two or three people trying to help him up.

— Don't look. Keep going, Arthur had said.

— He's lucky, having friends like you, Noreen said.

She worked at Grey Advertising, which made it so convenient to meet. Seeing her always filled him with pleasure, even when it became completely familiar. She was twenty-five and filled with life. That summer he saw her in a bathing suit, a bikini. She was stunning, with a kind of glow to her skin. She had a young girl's unself-conscious belly and ran into the waves. He went in more cautiously, as befitted a man who had been a typist in the army and salesman for a dress manufacturer before coming to what he called Wall Street, where he had always dreamed of being and would have worked for nothing.

The waves, the ocean, the white blinding sand. It was at Westhampton, where they went for the weekend. On the train every seat was taken. Young men in T-shirts and with manly chests were joking in the aisles. Noreen sat beside him, the happiness coming off her like heat. She had a small gold cross, the size of a dime, on a thin gold necklace lying on her shirt. He hadn't noticed it before. He was about to say something when the train began bucking and slowed to a stop.

— What is it? What's happened?

They were not in a station but alongside a low embankment, amid weedy-looking growth. After a while the word came back, they had hit a bicyclist.

— Where? How? Arthur said. We're in a forest.

No one knew much more. People were speculating, should they get off and try to find a taxi; where were they, anyhow? There were guesses. A few individuals did get off and were walking by the side of the train.

— God, I knew something like this would happen, Arthur said.

— Something like this? Noreen said. How could there be something like this?

— When we hit the cow, a man sitting across from them offered.

— The cow? We also hit a cow? Arthur exclaimed.

— A couple of weeks ago, the man explained.

That night Noreen showed him how to eat a lobster.

— My mother would die if she knew this, Arthur said.

— How will she know?

— She'd disown me.

— You start with the claws, Noreen said.

She had tucked the napkin into his collar. They drank some Italian wine.

Westhampton, her tanned legs and pale heels. The feeling she gave him of being younger, even, God help him, debonair. He was playful. On the beach he wore a coconut hat. He had fallen in love, deeply, and without knowing it. He hadn't realized he had been living a shallow life. He only knew that he was happy, happier than he had ever been, in her company. This warmhearted girl with her legs, her fragrance, and perfect little ears that were tuned to him. And she took some kind of pleasure in him! They were guests of the Senders and he slept in a separate room in the basement while she was upstairs, but they were under the same roof and he would see her in the morning.

— When are you going to marry her? everyone asked.

— She wouldn't have me, he equivocated.

Then, offhandedly, she admitted meeting someone else. It

was sort of a joke, Bobby Piro. He was stocky, he lived with his mother, had never married.

— He has black, shiny hair, Arthur guessed as if good-naturedly.

He had to treat it lightly, and Noreen did the same. She would make fun of Bobby when talking about him, his brothers, Dennis and Paul, his wanting to go to Vegas, his mother making chicken Vesuvio, Sinatra's favorite, for her.

— Chicken Vesuvio, Arthur said.

— It was pretty good.

— So you met his mother.

— I'm too skinny, she said.

— She sounds like my mother. Are you sure she's Italian?

She liked Bobby, at least a little, he could see. Still it was difficult to think of him as being really significant. He was someone to talk about. He wanted her to go away on a weekend with him.

— To the Euripides, Arthur said, his stomach suddenly turning over.

— Not that good.

The Euripides Hotel that didn't exist, but that they always joked about because he didn't know who Euripides was.

— Don't let him take you to the Euripides, he said.

— I couldn't do that. It's a Greek place, she said. For us Greeks.

Then, late one night in October, his doorbell rang.

— Who is it? Arthur said.

— It's me.

He opened the door. She stood in the doorway with a smile that he saw had hesitation in it.

— Can I come in?

— Sure, tootsula. Of course. Come in. What's happened, is something wrong?

— There's nothing wrong, really. I just thought I would . . . come by.

The room was clean but somehow barren. He never sat in it and as much as read a book. He lived in the bedroom like a salesman. The curtains hadn't been washed in a long time.

— Here, sit down, he said.

She was walking a bit carefully. She had been drinking, he could see. She felt her way around a chair and sat.

— You want something? Coffee? I'll make some coffee.

She was looking around her.

— You know, I've never been here. This is the first time.

— It's not much of a place. I guess I could find something better.

— Is that the bedroom?

— Yes, he said, but her gaze had drifted from it.

— I just wanted to talk.

— Sure. About what?

He knew, or was afraid he did.

— We've known each other a long time. What has it been, three years?

He felt nervous. The aimless way it was going. He didn't want to disappoint her. On the other hand, he was not sure what it was she wanted. Him? Now?

— You're pretty smart, she said.

— Me? Oh, God, no.

— You understand people. Can you really make some coffee? I think I'd like a cup.

While he busied himself, she sat quietly. He glanced briefly and saw her staring toward the window, beyond which were the lights of apartments in other buildings and the black, starless sky.

— So, she said, holding the coffee, give me some advice. Bobby wants to get married.

Arthur was silent.

— He wants to marry me. The reason I was never serious about him, I was always making fun of him, his being so Italian, his big smile, the reason was that he was involved all that time with some Danish girl. Ode is her name.

— I figured something like that.

— What did you figure?

— Ah, I could see something wasn't right.

— I never met her. I imagined her as being pretty and having this great accent. You know how you torture yourself.

— Ah, Noreen, he said. There's nobody nicer than you.

— Anyway, yesterday he told me he'd broken up with her. It was all over. He did it because of me. He realized it was me he loved, and he wanted to marry me.

— Well, that's . . .

Arthur didn't know what to say; his thoughts were skipping wildly, like scraps of paper in a wind. There is that fearful moment in the ceremony when it is asked if there is anyone who knows why these two should not be wed. This was that moment.

— What did you tell him?

— I haven't told him.

A gulf was opening between them somehow. It was happening as they sat there.

— Do you have any feeling about it? she asked.

— Yes, I mean, I'd like to think about it. It's kind of a surprise.

— It was to me, too.

She hadn't touched the coffee.

— You know, I could sit here for a long time, she said. It's as comfortable as I'll ever feel anywhere. That's what's making me wonder. About what to tell him.

— I'm a little afraid, he said. I can't explain it.

— Of course you are. Her voice had such understanding. Really. I know.

— Your coffee's going to get cold, he said.

— Anyway, I just wanted to see your apartment, she said. Her voice suddenly sounded funny. She seemed not to want to go on.

He realized then, as she sat there, a woman in his apartment at night, a woman he knew he loved, that she was really giving him one last chance. He knew he should take it.

— Ah, Noreen, he said.

After that night, she vanished. Not suddenly, but it did not take long. She married Bobby. It was as simple as a death, but it lasted longer. It seemed it would never go away. She lingered in his thoughts. Did he exist in hers? he often wondered. Did she still feel, even if only a little, the way he felt? The years seemed to have no effect on it. She was in New Jersey somewhere, in some place he could not picture. Probably there was a family. Did she ever think of him? Ah, Noreen.

SHE HAD NOT CHANGED. He could tell it from her voice, speaking, as always, to him alone.

— You probably have kids, he said as if casually.

— He didn't want them. Just one of the problems. Well, all that's *acqua passata*, as he liked to say. You didn't know I got divorced?

— No.

— I more or less kept in touch with Marie up until she retired. She told me how you were doing. You're a big wheel now.

— Not really.

— I knew you would be. It would be nice to see you again. How long has it been?

— Gee, a long time.

— You ever go out to Westhampton?

— No, not for years.

— Goldie's?

— He closed.

— I guess I knew that. Those were wonderful days.

It was the same, the ease of talking to her. He saw her great, winning smile, the well-being of it, her carefree walk.

— I'd love to see you, she said again.

They agreed to meet at the Plaza. She was going to be near there the next day.

He began walking up Fifth a little before five. He felt uncertain but tenderhearted, in the hands of a wondrous fate. The hotel stood before him, immense and vaguely white. He walked up the broad steps. There was a kind of foyer with a large table and flowers, the sound of people talking. As if, like an animal, he could detect the slightest noise, he seemed to make out the clink of cups and spoons.

There were flower boxes with pink flowers, the tall columns with their gilded tops, and in the Palm Court itself, which was crowded, through a glass panel he saw her sitting in a chair. For a moment he was not sure it was her. He moved away. Had she seen him?

He could not go in. He turned instead and went down the corridor to the men's room. An old man in black pants and a striped vest, the attendant, offered a towel as Arthur looked at himself in the long mirror to see if he had changed that much, too. He saw a man of fifty-five with the same Coney Island face he had always seen, half comic, kind. No worse than that. He gave the attendant a dollar and walked into the Palm Court, where, amid the chattering tables, the mock candelabra, and illuminated ceiling, Noreen was waiting. He was wearing his familiar dog's smile.

— Arthur, God, you look exactly the same. You haven't changed a bit, she said enthusiastically. I wish I could say that.

It was hard to believe. She was twenty years older; she had gained weight, even her face showed it. She had been the most beautiful girl.

— You look great, he said. I'd recognize you anywhere.

— Life's been good to you, she said.

— Well, I can't complain.

— I guess I can't either. What happened to everybody?

— What do you mean?

— Morris?

— He died. Five or six years ago.

— That's too bad.

— They gave him a big dinner before that. He was all smiles.

— You know, I've wanted to talk to you so much. I wanted to

call you, but I was involved in all this tedious divorce stuff. Anyway, I'm finally free. I should have taken your advice.

— What was that?

— Not to marry him, she said.

— I said that?

— No, but I could see you didn't like him.

— I was jealous of him.

— Truly?

— Sure. I mean, let's face it.

She smiled at him.

— Isn't it funny, she said, five minutes with you and it's as if none of it ever happened.

Her clothes, he noticed, even her clothes were hiding who she had been.

— Love never dies, he said.

— Do you mean that?

— You know that.

— Listen, can you have dinner?

— Ah, sweetheart, he said, I'd love to, but I can't. I don't know if you knew this, but I'm engaged.

— Well, congratulations, she said. I didn't know.

He had no idea what had made him say it. It was a word he had never used before in his life.

— That's wonderful, she said straightforwardly, smiling at him with such understanding that he was sure she had seen through him, but he could not imagine them walking into Clarke's, like an old couple, a couple from time past.

— I figured it's time to settle down, he said.

— Of course.

She was not looking at him. She was studying her hands.

Then she smiled again. She was forgiving him, he felt. That was it. She always understood.

They talked on, but not about much.

He left through the same foyer with its worn mosaic tile and people coming in. It was still light outside, the pure full light before evening, the sun in a thousand windows facing the park. Walking along the street in their heels, alone or together, were girls such as Noreen had been, many of them. They were not really going to meet for lunch sometime. He thought of the love that had filled the great central chamber of his life and how he would not meet anyone like that again. He did not know what came over him, but on the street he broke into tears.

Bangkok

———————◆———————

HOLLIS WAS IN THE BACK at a table piled with books and a space among them where he was writing when Carol came in.

— Hello, she said.

— Well, look who's here, he said coolly. Hello.

She was wearing a gray jersey sweater and a narrow skirt; as always, dressed well.

— Didn't you get my message? she asked.

— Yes.

— You didn't call back.

— No.

— Weren't you going to?

— Of course not, he said.

He looked wider than the last time and his hair, halfway to the shoulder, needed to be cut.

— I went by your apartment but you'd gone. I talked to Pam, that's her name, isn't it? Pam.

— Yes.

— We talked. Not that long. She didn't seem interested in talking. Is she shy?

— No, she's not shy.

— I asked her a question. Want to know what it was?

— Not especially, he said.

He leaned back. His jacket was draped over the back of the chair and his sleeves rolled partway up. She noticed a round wristwatch with a brown leather strap.

— I asked her if you still liked to have your cock sucked.

— Get out of here, he ordered. Go on, get out.

— She didn't answer, Carol said.

He had a moment of fear, of guilt almost, about consequences. On the other hand, he didn't believe her.

— So, do you? she said.

— Leave, will you? Please, he said in a civilized tone. He made a dispersing motion with his hand. I mean it.

— I'm not going to stay long, just a few minutes. I wanted to see you, that's all. Why didn't you call back?

She was tall with a long, elegant nose like a thoroughbred's. What people look like isn't the same as what you remember. She had been coming out of a restaurant one time, down some steps long after lunch in a silk dress that clung around the hips and the wind pulled against her legs. The afternoons, he thought for a moment.

She sat down in the leather chair opposite and gave a slight, uncertain smile.

— You have a nice place.

It had the makings of one, two rooms on the garden floor with a little grass and the backs of discrete houses behind, though there was just one window and the floorboards were worn. He sold fine books and manuscripts, letters for the most part, and had too big an inventory for a dealer his size.

After ten years in retail clothing he had found his true life. The rooms had high ceilings, the bookcases were filled and against them, on the floor, a few framed photographs leaned.

— Chris, she said, tell me something. Whatever happened to that picture of us taken at that lunch Diana Wald gave at her mother's house that day? Up there on that fake hill made from all the old cars? Do you still have that?

— It must have gotten lost.

— I'd really like to have it. It was a wonderful picture. Those were the days, she said. Do you remember the boat house we had?

— Of course.

— I wonder if you remember it the way I remember it.

— That would be hard to say. He had a low, persuasive voice. There was confidence in it, perhaps a little too much.

— The pool table, do you remember that? And the bed by the windows.

He didn't answer. She picked up one of the books from the table and was looking through it; *e.e. cummings*, The Enormous Room, *dust jacket with some small chips at bottom, minor soil on title page, otherwise very good. First edition.* The price was marked in pencil on the corner of the flyleaf at the top. She turned the pages idly.

— This has that part in it you like so much. What is it, again?

— Jean Le Nègre.

— That's it.

— Still unrivaled, he said.

— Makes me think of Alan Baron for some reason. Are you still in touch with him? Did he ever publish anything? Always telling me about Tantric yoga and how I should try it. He wanted to show it to me.

— So, did he?

— You're kidding.

She was leafing through the pages with her long thumbs.

— They're always talking about Tantric yoga, she said, or telling you about their big dicks. Not you, though. So, how is Pam, incidentally? I couldn't really tell. Is she happy?

— She's very happy.

— That's nice. And you have a little girl now, how old is she again?

— Her name is Chloe. She's six.

— Oh, she's big. They know a lot at that age, don't they? They know and they don't know, she said. She closed the book and put it down. Their bodies are so pure. Does Chloe have a nice body?

— You'd kill for it, he said casually.

— A perfect little body. I can picture it. Do you give her baths? I bet you do. You're a model father, the father every little girl ought to have. How will you be when she's bigger, I wonder? When the boys start coming around.

— There're not going to be a lot of boys coming around.

— Oh, for God's sake. Of course, there will. They'll be coming around just quivering. You know that. She'll have breasts and that first, soft pubic hair.

— You know, Carol, you're disgusting.

— You don't like to think of it, that's all. But she's going to be a woman, you know, a young woman. You remember how you felt about young women at that age. Well, it didn't all stop with you. It continues, and she'll be part of it, perfect body and all. How is Pam's, by the way?

— How's yours?

— Can't you tell?

— I wasn't paying attention.

— Do you still have sex? she asked unconcernedly.

— There are times.

— I don't. Rarely.

— That's a little hard to believe.

— It never measures up, that's the trouble. It's never what it should be or used to be. How old are you now? You look a little heavier. Do you exercise? Do you go to the steam room and look down at yourself?

— I don't have the time.

— Well, if you *had* more time. If you were free you'd be able to steam, shower, put on fresh clothes, and, let's see, not too early to go down to, what, the Odeon and have a drink and see if anyone's there, any girls. You could have the bartender offer them a drink or simply talk to them yourself, ask if they were doing anything for dinner, if they had any plans. As easy as that. You always liked good teeth. You liked slim arms and, how to put it, great tits, not necessarily big—good-sized, that's all. And long legs. Do you still like to tie their hands? You used to like to, it's always exciting to find out if they'll let you do it or not. Tell me, Chris, did you love me?

— Love you? He was leaning back in the chair. For the first time she had the impression he might have been drinking a little more than usual these days. Just the look of his face. I thought about you every minute of the day, he said. I loved everything you did. What I liked was that you were absolutely new and everything you said and did was. You were incomparable. With you I felt I had everything in life, everything anyone ever dreamed of. I adored you.

— Like no other woman?

— There was no one even close. I could have feasted on you forever. You were the intended.

— And Pam? You didn't feast on her?

— A little. Pam is something different.

— In what way?

— Pam doesn't take all that and offer it to someone else. I don't come back from a trip unexpectedly and find an unmade bed where you and some guy have been having a lovely time

— It wasn't that lovely.

— That's too bad.

— It was far from lovely.

— So, why did you do it, then?

— I don't know. I just had the foolish impulse to try something different. I didn't know that real happiness lies in having the same thing all the time.

She looked at her hands. He noticed again her long, flexible thumbs.

— Isn't that right? she asked coolly.

— Don't be nasty. Anyway, what do you know about true happiness?

— Oh, I've had it.

— Really?

— Yes, she said. With you.

He looked at her. She did not return his look, nor was she smiling.

— I'm going to Bangkok, she said. Well, Hong Kong first. Have you ever stayed at the Peninsula Hotel?

— I've never been to Hong Kong.

— They say it's the greatest hotel anywhere, Berlin, Paris, Tokyo.

— Well, I wouldn't know.

— You've been to hotels. Remember Venice and that little hotel by the theater? The water in the street up to your knees?

— I have a lot of work to do, Carol.

— Oh, come on.

— I have a business.

— Then how much is this e.e. cummings? she said. I'll buy it and you can take a few minutes off.

— It's already sold, he said.

— Still has the price in it.

He shrugged a little.

— Answer me about Venice, she said.

— I remember the hotel. Now let's say good-bye.

— I'm going to Bangkok with a friend.

He felt a phantom skip of the heart, however slight.

— Good, he said.

— Molly. You'd like her.

— Molly.

— We're traveling together. You know Daddy died.

— I didn't know that.

— Yes, a year ago. He died. So my worries are over. It's a nice feeling.

— I suppose. I liked your father.

He'd been a man in the oil business, sociable, with certain freely admitted prejudices. He wore expensive suits and had been divorced twice but managed to avoid loneliness.

— We're going to stay in Bangkok for a couple of months, perhaps come back through Europe, Carol said. Molly has a lot of style. She was a dancer. What was Pam, wasn't she a teacher or something? Well, you love Pam, you'd love Molly. You don't know her, but you would. She paused. Why don't you come with us? she said.

Hollis smiled slightly.

— Shareable, is she? he said.

— You wouldn't have to share.

It was meant to torment him, he knew.

— Leave my family and business, just like that?

— Gauguin did it.

— I'm a little more responsible than that. Maybe it's something you would do.

— If it were a choice, she said. Between life and . . .

— What?

— Life and a kind of pretend life. Don't act as if you didn't understand. There's nobody that understands better than you.

He felt an unwanted resentment. That the hunt be over, he thought. That it be ended. He heard her continue.

— Travel. The Orient. The air of a different world. Bathe, drink, read . . .

— You and me.

— And Molly. As a gift.

— Well, I don't know. What does she look like?

— She's good-looking, what would you expect? I'll undress her for you.

— I'll tell you something funny, Hollis said, something I heard. They say that everything in the universe, the planets, all the galaxies, everything—the entire universe—came originally from something the size of a grain of rice that exploded and formed what we have now, the sun, stars, earth, seas, everything there is, including what I felt for you. That morning on Hudson Street, sitting there in the sunlight, feet up, fulfilled and knowing it, talking, in love with one another—I knew I had everything life would ever offer.

— You felt that?

— Of course. Anyone would. I remember it all, but I can't feel it now. It's passed.

— That's sad.

— I have something more than that now. I have a wife I love and a kid.

— It's such a cliché, isn't it? A wife I love.

— It's just the truth.

— And you're looking forward to the years together, the ecstasy.

— It's not ecstasy.

— You're right.

— You can't have ecstasy daily.

— No, but you can have something as good, she said. You can have the anticipation of it.

— Good. Go ahead and have it. You and Molly.

— I'll think of you, Chris, in the house we'll have on the river in Bangkok.

— Oh, don't bother.

— I'll think of you lying in bed at night, bored to death with it all.

— Quit it, for God's sake. Leave it alone. Let me like you a little bit.

— I don't want you to like me. In a half-whisper she said, I want you to curse me.

— Keep it up.

— It's so sweet, she said. The little family, the lovely books. All right, then. You missed your chance. Bye-bye. Go back and give her a bath, your little girl. While you still can, anyway.

She looked at him a last time from the doorway. He could hear the sound of her heels as she went through the front room. He could hear them go past the display cases and toward the door where they seemed to hesitate, then the door closing.

The room was swimming, he could not hold on to his thoughts. The past, like a sudden tide, had swept back over him, not as it had been but as he could not help remembering it. The best thing was to resume work. He knew what her skin felt like, it was silky. He should not have listened.

On the soft, silent keys he began to write: *Jack Kerouac, typed letter signed ("Jack"), 1 page, to his girlfriend, the poet Lois Sorrells, single-spaced, signed in pencil, slight crease from folding.* It was not a pretend life.

Arlington

———◆———

NEWELL HAD MARRIED a Czech girl and they were having trouble, they were drinking and fighting. This was in Kaiserslautern and families in the building had complained. Westerveldt, who was acting adjutant, was sent to straighten things out—he and Newell had been classmates, though Newell was not someone in the class you remembered. He was quiet and kept to himself. He had an odd appearance, with a high, domed forehead and pale eyes. Jana, the wife, had a downturned mouth and nice breasts. Westerveldt didn't really know her. He knew her by sight.

Newell was in the living room when Westerveldt came by. He seemed unsurprised by the visit.

— I thought I might talk to you a little, Westerveldt said.

There was a slight nod.

— Is your wife here?

— I think she's in the kitchen.

— It's not really my business, but are the two of you having problems?

Newell seemed to be considering.

— Nothing serious, he finally said.

In the kitchen the Czech wife had her shoes off and was painting her toenails. She looked up briefly when Westerveldt came in. He saw the exotic, European mouth.

— I wonder if we could talk for a minute.

— About what? she said. There was uneaten food on the counter and unwashed dishes.

— Why don't you come into the living room?

She said nothing.

— Just for a couple of minutes.

She looked closely at her feet, ignoring him. Westerveldt had grown up with three sisters and was at ease around women. He touched her elbow to coax her but she jerked it away.

— Who are you? she said.

Westerveldt went back into the living room and talked to Newell like a brother. If this went on with him and his wife, it was jeopardizing his career.

Newell wanted to confide in Westerveldt. He sat silent, however, unable to begin. He was helplessly in love with this woman. When she dressed up she was simply beautiful. If you saw them together in the Wienerstube, his round white brow gleaming in the light and her across from him, smoking, you would wonder, how did he ever get her? She was insolent but there were times when she was not. To put your hand on the small of her naked back was to have all you ever hoped to possess.

— What is it that's bothering her? Westerveldt wanted to know.

— She's had a terrible life, Newell said. Everything will be all right.

114

Whatever else was said, Westerveldt didn't remember. What happened afterward erased it.

Newell was away on temporary duty somewhere and his wife, who had no friends, was bored. She went to the movies and wandered around in town. She went to the officers' club and sat at the bar, drinking. On Saturday she was there, bare shouldered, still drinking when the bar closed. The club officer, Captain Dardy, noticed it and asked if she needed someone to drive her home. He told her to wait a few minutes until he was finished closing up.

Early in the morning, in the gray light, Dardy's car was still parked outside the quarters. Jana could see it and so could everyone else. She leaned over and shook him and told him he had to leave.

— What time is it?

— I don't care. You have to go, she said.

Afterward she went to the military police and reported she had been raped.

IN HIS LONG, ADMIRED CAREER, Westerveldt had been like a figure in a novel. In the elephant grass near Pleiku he'd gotten a wide scar through one eyebrow where a mortar fragment, half an inch lower and a little closer, would have blinded or killed him. If anything, it enhanced his appearance. He'd had a long love affair with a woman in Naples when he'd been stationed there, a marquesa, in fact. If he resigned his commission and married her, she would buy him whatever he wanted. He could even have a mistress. That was just one episode. Women always liked him. In the end he married a woman from San Antonio, a divorcée with a child, and they had two more together. He was fifty-eight when he died from some kind of leukemia that began as a strange rash on his neck.

The chapel, an ordinary room with red wallpaper and benches, in the funeral home was crowded. Someone was delivering a eulogy, but in the corridor where many people stood it was hard to make out.

— Can you hear what he's saying?

— Nobody can, the man in front of Newell said. It was Bressi, he realized, Bressi with his hair now white.

— Are you going to the cemetery? Newell asked when the service was over.

— I'll give you a ride, Bressi told him.

They drove through Alexandria, the car full.

— There's the church that George Washington attended when he was president, Bressi said. A little later, he said, There's Robert E. Lee's boyhood home.

Bressi and his wife lived in Alexandria in a white clapboard house with a narrow front porch and black shutters.

— Who said, "Let us cross the river and rest in the shade of the trees"? he asked them.

No one answered. Newell felt their disdain for him. They were looking away, out the car windows.

— Anybody know? Bressi said. Lee's greatest tactical commander.

— Shot by his own men, Newell said, almost inaudibly.

— Mistakenly.

— At Chancellorsville, in the dusk.

— It's not far from here, about thirty miles, Bressi said. He had been first in military history. He glanced in the rearview mirror. How did you happen to know that? Where did you stand in military history?

Newell didn't answer.

No one spoke.

There was a long line of cars moving slowly, going into the cemetery. People who had already parked walked alongside them. There were more gravestones than one could believe.

Bressi extended an arm and, waving lightly toward an area, said something Newell could not hear. Thill is in that section somewhere, Bressi had said, referring to a Medal of Honor winner.

They walked with many others, toward the end drawn by faint music as if coming from the ancient river itself, the last river, the boatman waiting. The band, in dark blue uniforms, had formed in a small valley. It was playing "Wagon Wheels," *Carry me home* ... The grave was nearby, the fresh earth under a green tarpaulin.

Newell walked as if in a dream. He knew the men around him, but not really. He stopped at a gravestone for Westerveldt's father and mother, died thirty years apart, buried side by side.

There were faces he thought he recognized during the proceedings, which were long. A thick, folded flag was given to what must have been the widow and her children. Carrying yellow flowers with long stems they filed past the coffin, the family and also others. On an impulse, Newell followed them.

Volleys were being fired. A lone bugle, silvery and pure, began to play taps, the sound drifting over the hills. The retired generals and colonels stood, each with a hand held over his heart. They had served everywhere, though none of them had served time in prison as Newell had. The rape charge against Dardy had been dropped after an investigation, and with Westerveldt's help Newell had been transferred so he could make another start. Then Jana's parents in Czechoslovakia needed help and Newell, still a first lieutenant, finally managed to get the money to send to them. Her gratitude was heartfelt.

— Oh, God. I love you! she said.

Naked she sat astride him and, caressing her own buttocks as he lay nearly fainting, began to ride. A night he would never forget. Later there was the charge of having sold radios taken from supply. He was silent at the court-martial. Above all he wished he hadn't had to be there in uniform, it was like a crown of thorns. He had traded it and the silver bars and class ring to possess her. Of the three letters to the court appealing for leniency and attesting to his character, one was from Westerveldt.

Though the sentence was only a year, Jana did not wait for him. She went off with a man named Rodriguez who owned some beauty parlors. She was still young, she said.

The woman Newell later married knew nothing of all that or almost nothing. She was older than he was with two grown children and bad feet, she could walk only short distances, from the car to the supermarket. She knew he had been in the army—there were some photographs of him in uniform, taken years before,

— This is you, she said. So, what were you?

Newell hadn't walked back with the others, He had no excuse to do that. This was Arlington and here they all lay, formed up for the last time. He could almost hear the distant notes of adjutant's call. He walked in the direction of the road they had come in on. With a sound at first faint but then clopping rhythmically he heard the hooves of horses, a team of six black horses with three erect riders and the now-empty caisson that had carried the coffin, the large spoked wheels rattling on the road. The riders, in their dark caps, did not look at him. The gravestones in dense, unbroken lines curved along the hillsides and down toward the river, as far as he could see, all the same height with here and there a larger, gray stone like an officer, mounted, amid the ranks. In the fading light they seemed to be waiting, fateful, massed as if for some great assault. For a moment he felt exalted by it, by the thought of all these dead, the history of the nation, its people. It was hard to get into Arlington. He would never lie there; he had given that up long ago. He would never know the days with Jana again, either. He remembered her at that moment as she had been, when she was so slender and young. He was loyal to her. It was one-sided, but that was enough.

When at the end they had all stood with their hands over their hearts, Newell was to one side, alone, resolutely saluting, faithful, like the fool he had always been.

Last Night

WALTER SUCH was a translator. He liked to write with a green fountain pen that he had a habit of raising in the air slightly after each sentence, almost as if his hand were a mechanical device. He could recite lines of Blok in Russian and then give Rilke's translation of them in German, pointing out their beauty. He was a sociable but also sometimes prickly man, who stuttered a little at first and who lived with his wife in a manner they liked. But Marit, his wife, was ill.

He was sitting with Susanna, a family friend. Finally, they heard Marit on the stairs, and she came into the room. She was wearing a red silk dress in which she had always been seductive, with her loose breasts and sleek, dark hair. In the white wire baskets in her closet were stacks of folded clothes, underwear, sport things, nightgowns, the shoes jumbled beneath on the floor. Things she would never again need. Also jewelry, bracelets and necklaces, and a lacquer box with all her rings. She had looked through the lacquer box at length and picked several. She didn't want her fingers, bony now, to be naked.

— You look re-really nice, her husband said.

— I feel as if it's my first date or something. Are you having a drink?

— Yes.

— I think I'll have one. Lots of ice, she said.

She sat down.

— I have no energy, she said, that's the most terrible part. It's gone. It doesn't come back. I don't even like to get up and walk around.

— It must be very difficult, Susanna said.

— You have no idea.

Walter came back with the drink and handed it to his wife.

— Well, happy days, she said. Then, as if suddenly remembering, she smiled at them. A frightening smile. It seemed to mean just the opposite.

It was the night they had decided would be the one. On a saucer in the refrigerator, the syringe lay. Her doctor had supplied the contents. But a farewell dinner first, if she were able. It should not be just the two of them, Marit had said. Her instinct. They had asked Susanna rather than someone closer and grief-filled, Marit's sister, for example, with whom she was not on good terms, anyway, or older friends. Susanna was younger. She had a wide face and high, pure forehead. She looked like the daughter of a professor or banker, slightly errant. Dirty girl, one of their friends had commented about her, with a degree of admiration.

Susanna, sitting in a short skirt, was already a little nervous. It was hard to pretend it would be just an ordinary dinner. It would be hard to be offhanded and herself. She had come as dusk was falling. The house with its lighted windows—every room seemed to be lit—had stood out from all the others like a place in which something festive was happening.

Marit gazed at things in the room, the photographs with their silver frames, the lamps, the large books on Surrealism, landscape design, or country houses that she had always meant to sit down with and read, the chairs, even the rug with its beautiful faded color. She looked at it all as if she were somehow noting it, when in fact it all meant nothing. Susanna's long hair and freshness meant something, though she was not sure what.

Certain memories are what you long to take with you, she thought, memories from even before Walter, from when she was a girl. Home, not this one but the original one with her childhood bed, the window on the landing out of which she had watched the swirling storms of long-ago winters, her father bending over her to say good night, the lamplight in which her mother was holding out a wrist, trying to fasten a bracelet.

That home. The rest was less dense. The rest was a long novel so like your life; you were going through it without thinking and then one morning it ended: there were bloodstains.

— I've had a lot of these, Marit reflected.

— The drink? Susanna said.

— Yes.

— Over the years, you mean.

— Yes, over the years. What time is it getting to be?

— Quarter to eight, her husband said.

— Shall we go?

— Whenever you like, he said. No need to hurry.

— I don't want to hurry.

She had, in fact, little desire to go. It was one step closer.

— What time is the reservation? she asked.

— Any time we like.

— Let's go, then.

It was in the uterus and had travelled from there to the lungs. In the end, she had accepted it. Above the square neckline of her dress the skin, pallid, seemed to emanate a darkness. She no longer resembled herself. What she had been was gone; it had been taken from her. The change was fearful, especially in her face. She had a face now that was for the afterlife and those she would meet there. It was hard for Walter to remember how she had once been. She was almost a different woman from the one to whom he had made a solemn promise to help when the time came.

Susanna sat in the back as they drove. The roads were empty. They passed houses showing a shifting, bluish light downstairs. Marit sat silent. She felt sadness but also a kind of confusion. She was trying to imagine all of it tomorrow, without her being here to see it. She could not imagine it. It was difficult to think the world would still be there.

At the hotel, they waited near the bar, which was noisy. Men without jackets, girls talking or laughing loudly, girls who knew nothing. On the walls were large French posters, old lithographs, in darkened frames.

— I don't recognize anyone, Marit commented. Luckily, she added.

Walter had seen a talkative couple they knew, the Apthalls.

— Don't look, he said. They haven't seen us. I'll get a table in the other room.

— Did they see us? Marit asked as they were seated. I don't feel like talking to anyone.

— We're all right, he said.

The waiter was wearing a white apron and black bow tie. He handed them the menu and a wine list.

— Can I get you something to drink?

— Yes, definitely, Walter said.

He was looking at the list, on which the prices were in roughly ascending order. There was a Cheval Blanc for five hundred and seventy-five dollars.

— This Cheval Blanc, do you have this?

— The 1989? the waiter asked.

— Bring us a bottle of that.

— What is Cheval Blanc? Is it a white? Susanna asked when the waiter had gone.

— No, it's a red, Walter said.

— You know, it was very nice of you to join us tonight, Marit said to Susanna. It's quite a special evening.

— Yes.

— We don't usually order wine this good, she explained.

The two of them had often eaten here, usually near the bar, with its gleaming rows of bottles. They had never ordered wine that cost more than thirty-five dollars.

How was she feeling, Walter asked while they waited. Was she feeling OK?

— I don't know how to express how I'm feeling. I'm taking morphine, Marit told Susanna. It's doing the job, but . . . she stopped. There are a lot of things that shouldn't happen to you, she said.

Dinner was quiet. It was difficult to talk casually. They had

two bottles of the wine, however. He would never drink this
well again, Walter could not help thinking. He poured the last
of the second bottle into Susanna's glass.

— No, you should drink it, she said. It's really for you.

— He's had enough, Marit said. It was good, though,
wasn't it?

— Fabulously good.

— Makes you realize there are things . . . oh, I don't know,
various things. It would be nice to have always drunk it. She
said it in a way that was enormously touching.

They were all feeling better. They sat for a while and finally
made their way out. The bar was still noisy.

Marit stared out the window as they drove. She was tired.
They were going home now. The wind was moving in the tops
of the shadowy trees. In the night sky there were brilliant
blue clouds, shining as if in daylight.

— It's very beautiful tonight, isn't it? Marit said. I'm struck
by that. Am I mistaken?

— No. Walter cleared his throat. It is beautiful.

— Have you noticed it? she asked Susanna. I'm sure you
have. How old are you? I forget.

— Twenty-nine.

— Twenty-nine, Marit said. She was silent for a few moments. We never had children, she said. Do you wish you had
children?

— Oh, sometimes, I suppose. I haven't thought about it too
much. It's one of those things you have to be married to really
think about.

— You'll be married.

— Yes, perhaps.

— You could be married in a minute, Marit said.

She was tired when they reached the house. They sat together in the living room as if they had come from a big party but were not quite ready for bed. Walter was thinking of what lay ahead, the light that would come on in the refrigerator when the door was opened. The needle of the syringe was sharp, the stainless-steel point cut at an angle and like a razor. He was going to have to insert it into her vein. He tried not to dwell on it. He would manage somehow. He was becoming more and more nervous.

— I remember my mother, Marit said. She wanted to tell me things at the end, things that had happened when I was young. Rae Mahin had gone to bed with Teddy Hudner. Anne Herring had, too. They were married women. Teddy Hudner wasn't married. He worked in advertising and was always playing golf. My mother went on like that, who slept with whom. That's what she wanted to tell me, finally. Of course, at the time, Rae Mahin was really something.

Then Marit said,

— I think I'll go upstairs.

She stood up.

— I'm all right, she told her husband. Don't come up just yet. Good night, Susanna.

When there were just the two of them, Susanna said,

— I have to go.

— No, don't. Please don't go. Stay here.

She shook her head.

— I can't, she said.

— Please, you have to. I'm going to go upstairs in a little while, but when I come down I can't be alone. Please.

There was silence.

— Susanna.

They sat without speaking.

— I know you've thought all this out, she said.

— Yes, absolutely.

After a few minutes, Walter looked at his watch; he began to say something but then did not. A little later, he looked at it again, then left the room.

The kitchen was in the shape of an L, old-fashioned and unplanned, with a white enamel sink and wooden cabinets painted many times. In the summers they had made pre-serves here when boxes of strawberries were sold at the stairway going down to the train platform in the city, unfor-gettable strawberries, their fragrance like perfume. There were still some jars. He went to the refrigerator and opened the door.

There it was, the small etched lines on the side. There were ten ccs. He tried to think of a way not to go on. If he dropped the syringe, broke it somehow, and said his hand had been shaking . . .

He took the saucer and covered it with a dish towel. It was worse that way. He put it down and picked up the syringe, holding it in various ways—finally, almost concealed against his leg. He felt light as a sheet of paper, devoid of strength.

Marit had prepared herself. She had made up her eyes and put on an ivory satin nightgown, low in back. It was the gown she would be wearing in the next world. She had made an effort to believe in an afterworld. The crossing was by boat, something the ancients knew with certainty. Over her collar-bones lay strands of a silver necklace. She was weary. The wine had had an effect, but she was not calm.

In the doorway, Walter stood, as if waiting for permission.

She looked at him without speaking. He had it in his hand, she saw. Her heart skidded nervously, but she was determined not to show it.

— Well, darling, she said.

He tried to reply. She had on fresh lipstick, he saw; her mouth looked dark. There were some photographs she had arranged around her on the bed.

— Come in.

— No, I'll be back, he managed to say.

He hurried downstairs. He was going to fail; he had to have a drink. The living room was empty. Susanna had gone. He had never felt more completely alone. He went into the kitchen and poured some vodka, odorless and clear, into a glass and quickly drank it. He went slowly upstairs again and sat on the bed near his wife. The vodka was making him drunk. He felt unlike himself.

— Walter, she said.

— Yes?

— This is the right thing.

She reached to take his hand. Somehow it frightened him, as if it might mean an appeal to come with her.

— You know, she said evenly, I've loved you as much as I've ever loved anyone in the world—I'm sounding maudlin, I know.

— Ah, Marit! he cried.

— Did you love me?

His stomach was churning in despair.

— Yes, he said. Yes!

— Take care of yourself.

— Yes.

He was in good health, as it happened, a little heavier than he might have been, but nevertheless . . . His roundish, scholarly stomach was covered with a layer of soft, dark hair, his hands and nails well cared for.

She leaned forward and embraced him. She kissed him. For a moment, she was not afraid. She would live again, be young again as she once had been. She held out her arm. On the inside, two veins the color of verdigris were visible. He began to press to make them rise. Her head was turned away.

— Do you remember, she said to him, when I was working at Bates and we met that first time? I knew right away.

The needle was wavering as he tried to position it.

— I was lucky, she said. I was very lucky.

He was barely breathing. He waited, but she did not say anything more. Hardly believing what he was doing he pushed the needle in—it was effortless—and slowly injected the contents. He heard her sigh. Her eyes were closed as she lay back. Her face was peaceful. She had embarked. My God, he thought, my God. He had known her when she was in her twenties, long-legged and innocent. Now he had slipped her, as in a burial at sea, beneath the flow of time. Her hand was still warm. He took it and held it to his lips. He pulled the bedspread up to cover her legs. The house was incredibly quiet. It had fallen into silence, the silence of a fatal act. He could not hear the wind.

He went slowly downstairs. A sense of relief came over him, enormous relief and sadness. Outside, the monumental blue clouds filled the night. He stood for a few minutes and then saw, sitting in her car, motionless, Susanna. She rolled down the window as he approached.

— You didn't go, he said.

— I couldn't stay in there.

— It's over, he said. Come in. I'm going to get a drink.

She stood in the kitchen with him, her arms folded, a hand on each elbow.

— It wasn't terrible, he said. It's just that I feel . . . I don't know.

They drank standing there.

— Did she really want me to come? Susanna said.

— Darling, *she* suggested it. She didn't know a thing.

— I wonder.

— Believe me. Nothing.

She put down her drink.

— No, drink it, he said. It'll help.

— I feel funny.

— Funny? You're not feeling sick?

— I don't know.

— Don't be sick. Here, come with me. Wait, I'll get you some water.

She was concentrating on breathing evenly.

— You'd better lie down for a bit, he said.

— No, I'm all right.

— Come.

He led her, in her short skirt and blouse, to a room to one side of the front door and made her sit on the bed. She was taking slow breaths.

— Susanna.

— Yes.

— I need you.

She more or less heard him. Her head was thrown back like that of a woman longing for God.

— I shouldn't have drunk so much, she murmured.

He began to unbutton her blouse.

— No, she said, trying to rebutton it.

He was unfastening her brassiere. Her gorgeous breasts emerged. He could not take his eyes from them. He kissed them passionately. She felt herself moved to the side as he pulled down the cover of the white sheets. She tried to speak again, but he put his hand over her mouth and pushed her down. He devoured her, shuddering as if in fright at the end and holding her to him tightly. They fell into a profound sleep.

IN EARLIEST MORNING, light was clear and intensely bright. The house, standing in its path, became even whiter. It stood out from its neighbors, more pure and serene. The shadow of a tall elm beside it was traced on it as finely as if drawn by a pencil. The pale curtains hung unmoving. Nothing stirred within. In back was the wide lawn across which Susanna had been idly strolling as part of a garden tour on the day he had first seen her, shapely and tall. It was a vision he had not been able to erase, though the rest had started later, when she came to redo the garden with Marit.

They sat at the table drinking coffee. They were complicit, not long risen, and not regarding one another too closely. Walter was admiring her, however. Without makeup she was even more appealing. Her long hair was not combed. She seemed very approachable. There were calls that would have to be made, but he was not thinking of them. It was still too early. He was thinking past this day. Mornings to come. At first he hardly heard the sound behind him. It was a footstep

and then, slowly, another—Susanna turned white—as Marit
came unsteadily down the stairs. The makeup on her face
was stale, and her dark lipstick showed fissures. He stared in
disbelief.

— Something went wrong, she said.

— Are you all right? he asked foolishly.

— No, you must have done it wrong.

— Oh, God, Walter murmured.

She sat weakly on the bottom step. She did not seem to
notice Susanna.

— I thought you were going to help me, she said, and began
to cry.

— I can't understand it, he said.

— It's all wrong, Marit was repeating. Then, to Susanna,
You're still here?

— I was just leaving, Susanna said.

— I don't understand, Walter said again.

— I have to do it all over, Marit sobbed.

— I'm sorry, he said. I'm so sorry.

He could think of nothing more to say. Susanna had gone
to get her clothes. She left by the front door.

That was how she and Walter came to part, upon being
discovered by his wife. They met two or three times afterward, at his insistence, but to no avail. Whatever holds people
together was gone. She told him she could not help it. That
was just the way it was.

ACKNOWLEDGMENTS

With gratitude especially to Rust Hills, long the literary editor at *Esquire*, for his help and cherished friendship, and also to Terry McDonell. I am deeply indebted as well to Frank Conroy for the generosity and affection that provided me the chance to read some of these stories at the Writers' Workshop in Iowa.

picador.com

blog
videos
interviews
extracts